Bitter Waters

By
Patricia Hulsey

http://www.harvestime.org

Dedication

To Michelle
1968-1986

and

to my sister and her mother
Catherine Louise Thomas
who joined Michelle in Heaven
February, 1995

TABLE OF CONTENTS

To Michelle

February 1. This is your birthday. Birthdays are a time for beginnings, so on this day I begin your story.

It seems just days ago that I held in my arms the tiny bundle of life who was to be known as Michelle Louise Downs.

You were the child of my sister's natural womb. You became the child of my own spiritual womb.

The first time I held you, I prayed that if God had a purpose for our lives together He would create a special bond of love between us.

From the very beginning, it was always there. I remember how you would squeal with delight when I would come into the room, your dark eyes flashing and chubby brown arms extended towards me. But I did not really understand then the great purpose for which that bond of love was forged.

It has been said that no writer has ever written anything of significance unless the pen was dipped into his own life's blood-- until he has made bare his soul and spirit, drawing back the curtains from hidden pain and suffering to share openly with others.

This is such a story. It is written in your life's blood and birthed from the anguish of my own spirit. It is the story of *"Bitter Waters."*

It is your story--and yet--it is the story of many others...

To The Reader

This is the story of Michelle, but it is also *your* story...

- If you are facing the greatest challenge you have ever experienced.

- If you are engulfed with grief for a loved one.

- If you are facing the trauma of divorce.

- If you are depressed and discouraged.

- If you are facing death.

- If you have been rejected, abused, or abandoned.

- If you have questions for which there seems to be no answers...

...Then this is your story.

The difficulty you face is different because no painful experience is identical to another, other than in the fact that you are hurting. The details are not the same, by any means. But the basic problem is common.

You, too, stand on the banks of Bitter Waters.

Four Words That Changed The World

Spring had come early to the valley that year. The fields were emerald green and the fruit and nut trees of the surrounding farms were heavy with blossoms.

The blackberries had already ripened on the vine in the warm spring sun and I spent the afternoon filling buckets with the juicy fruit. It had been a pleasant day touched by joyful anticipation of the coming summer.

At 6 p.m. on May 22, 1986, the insistent ringing of the telephone shattered the quiet of the early spring evening. As I lifted the receiver, four words were spoken which were to change my world: "Seth has shot Michelle..."

The caller was my mother. Hysterically she repeated the urgent message. "Seth has shot Michelle. He shot her! With a gun!" [*]

Michelle was my niece. Seth was her fiancé. Their planned wedding was just days away.

"How did it happen? How badly is she hurt?," I questioned urgently.

---

[*] The names of people and places in this account are factual with the exception of one. The name "Seth" is used for Michelle's fiancé.

"I don't know. Cathy just called and she said is leaving El Paso for Portales," said Mom. Cathy was my sister and Michelle's mother.

"Patti, I don't know what happened. I don't know how bad she is hurt. I don't know anything!" Mom finished with a sob.

"Now Mom, don't get all upset." I tried to speak reassuringly, although tentacles of fear clutched at my heart and knotted somewhere in the depths of my being. "We don't know how badly she is hurt. It may be a minor incident. Let me see what I can find out."

I terminated the call abruptly and dialed information for Portales, New Mexico. "I need the telephone number for the hospital in Portales. No, I don't know its exact name. Operator--look, this is an emergency! Please, help me."

In just a few seconds I was dialing the number of the hospital with shaking fingers.

"Emergency room, please," I requested urgently. I waited as the call was transferred. The phone rang once, then twice.

"This is emergency," answered a crisp professional voice. "May I help you?"

"Yes, please! You have a gunshot victim that was just brought in. Her name is Michelle Downs. Please--I need to talk to someone who can tell me how she is. This is her aunt calling from California."

"Just a moment, ma'am." Seconds seemed like minutes until the calming voice of the doctor came on the line.

"We don't know how badly Michelle is injured," he answered my question honestly. "She was shot in the lower right side and we are presently trying to stabilize her. We won't know the extent of the injuries until we get her into surgery."

Then Michelle's Grandma Thomas came on the line. She had accompanied Michelle in the ambulance to the hospital.

"Patti, it doesn't look good. We don't know what happened or how it happened yet. But pray! Call everyone you know to pray. It's real bad!"

I hung up the phone and terror turned to tears. My husband enfolded me in his arms and we prayed together. We prayed fervently that God would guide the hands of the doctors and for strength for Michelle. We prayed that Michelle would be raised up to glorify His name.

...Then we waited for a miracle.

Another Night Of Waiting

A little over 18 years ago, at this same time of the evening, I was also waiting for news about Michelle. Mom and I were anxiously pacing the sterile hallways of La Mirada Community Hospital while Cathy labored to bring forth life.

Cathy is my half-sister with whom I was raised. We were both children of divorce, with separate fathers. Cathy's father had deserted her when she was just a baby. My father, who lived near us, tried his best to fill that void in her life.

Mom worked to support us, so Cathy and I were cared for by her mother, our Grandma Young. We were raised in church and attended Christian school. We both were blessed by the firm discipline and love of our grandmother.

I was already working and living on my own when Grandma Young passed away. Cathy was still in high school and after Grandma's death, she turned to the wrong crowd for comfort. She began to smoke, experiment with drugs, and to adopt what was known in the 1970s as the "hippie" lifestyle.

When Cathy became pregnant, her boyfriend insisted on an abortion. Although Cathy was young, confused, and in a difficult situation, it was an unacceptable alternative for her. She could not end a human life. She didn't really want the baby, but she would not kill it.

When Cathy told Mom she was pregnant, Mom was very upset. She agreed abortion was not the answer, but she and our longtime family doctor both urged Cathy to put the baby up for adoption.

At first, Cathy considered this option. She was young, single, and the idea of a lifetime commitment to a child frightened her. But as the baby continued to develop within her body, a special love began to grow for this little stranger struggling for life. Eventually she decided on a different alternative. She would keep this child.

When she announced her decision, Mom said, "Well if you do, it is your responsibility. I won't care for that baby. You will have to care for it. I think you are making the wrong decision. You are so young, not married, and have no stable job."

The baby's father was Hispanic, and Cathy was fair-skinned. Mom blatantly expressed another fear. "What if that baby comes out looking like a Mexican?"

Early in the evening of February 1, 1968, the call came. "Patti, this is Mom. Cathy has gone into labor and we are leaving for the hospital. We'll meet you there."

So we waited as minutes turned to hours. Dr. Bailey would emerge periodically from the delivery room to give us an update on Cathy's condition.

Finally at 9:42 p.m., a little girl was born. Before Dr. Bailey would let Cathy see her, he asked one more time.

"Cathy, are you sure you want to keep the baby?"

"Yes, I'm sure," she answered.

Then her arms enveloped the eight pound bundle which she named Michelle Louise Downs.

When Dr. Bailey came out in the hallway to announce the birth, before he could speak Mom asked, "Is it Mexican?"

"Mom, you didn't even ask if it is a boy or girl," I chided.

"Oh, all right! Is it a boy or girl and is it Mexican?"

Dr. Bailey knew my Mom well and ignored her prejudicial comment. He put his arm around her shoulder and answered simply, "It's a girl."

In a few minutes Mom and I were peering through the glass windows of the nursery at a small bundle of life wrapped in a pink blanket. She had olive skin, brown eyes, and an abundance of dark black hair.

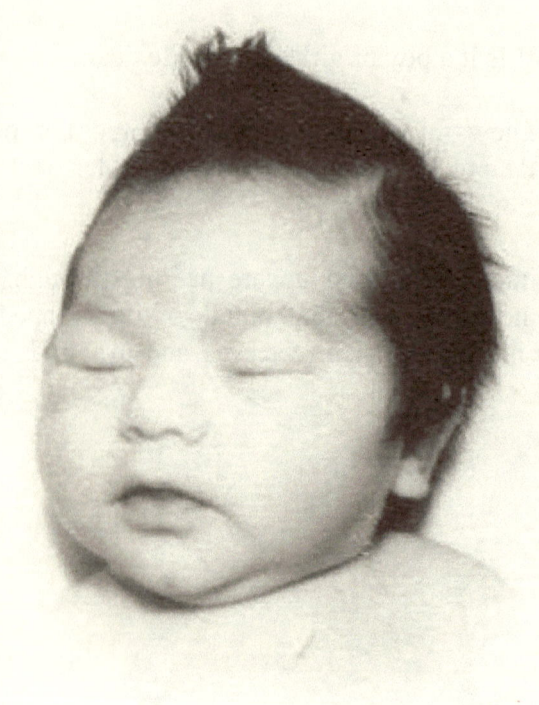

MICHELLE AT BIRTH

The Baby Nobody Wanted

Cathy lived temporarily at Mom's house until she could get a job and a place to live.

The day Cathy arrived home from the hospital was my first opportunity to hold Michelle. Unmarried at the time and never having been around new babies, I cautiously lifted her in my arms.

As I held the child, I prayed that if God had a purpose for me in her life He would forge a special bond of love between us. Suddenly I wanted very much to be there for this little baby that nobody wanted.

During the first month of Michelle's life, Mom was true to her word. She did not feed or change Michelle and had little more to do with her than to peer at her in the ruffled bassinet. But slowly the dark-haired baby with the toothless grin wrapped her chubby brown fingers around Mom's heart. Mom soon was answering Michelle's every cry. We had to wait our turn to feed and cuddle her!

Although Michelle's natural father never saw her and wanted nothing to do with her, Michelle immediately developed a special extended family. In addition to Mom, my step-dad Jerry, Cathy, and me, a dear friend named Janet became an adopted aunt to Michelle. Janet's mother, Jessie, became an adopted grandmother.

Years later, shortly before the tragic evening of May 22, 1986, Michelle wrote Aunt Janet...

> *Whether you know it or not, you are a big part of my life. Between you, Grandma Jessie, Aunt Patti, Jerry, and my own Grandma, I was the most cared for little girl in the world.*

The baby that nobody wanted became "the most cared for little girl in the world."

THE BABY NOBODY WANTED...
BECAME THE MOST CARED FOR LITTLE GIRL
IN THE WORLD

God's Little Creatures

Michelle was dressed in a frothy white lace dress which contrasted beautifully with her olive skin. She was held in the arms of a dear family friend, Rev. Valerie Howe.

In a little church in Los Nietos, California, Michelle was being dedicated to the Lord. As Rev. Howe held her up before the Lord, she quoted the words of Hannah in the Old Testament:

> *Therefore I give her to the Lord...as long as she lives she shall be lent to the Lord.*

It was a beautiful ceremony, but we would not really understand the true significance of these words of dedication until 18 years later.

Cathy got a job working at the local post office and moved into an apartment. Mom, Jerry, Aunt Janet, and I helped care for Michelle until she was old enough to enter the School For Beginning Years in Whittier.

On Michelle's first birthday, we had quite a celebration for someone who just one short year before had come into the world unplanned and unwanted.

Michelle wore a frilly blue organdy dress with long blue stockings. We had a cake decorated like a merry-go-round and she received a rocking horse, toy car, and a large stuffed tiger.

The video camera captured Michelle unceremoniously stuffing cake into her mouth with her chubby hands, with a good portion of the vanilla ice cream matted in her dark, thick hair.

Easter followed shortly thereafter, and Michelle wore a beautiful little pink bonnet and coat to the service commemorating the resurrection of Jesus. After church, the video camera was brought out again and we filmed her running up and down the walkway in front of my apartment, laughing with delight, so full of life.

Michelle had a slight deformity in her hip at birth which necessitated her sleeping in braces during the first two years of her life. At first she would put up an awful protest when the uncomfortable contraption was strapped on her little body.

But when we promised a special candy treat, she wore the braces without complaint. Michelle soon came to look forward to the evening ritual of the "candy bar shoes" as she promptly dubbed them.

True to my prayer, God forged a special bond of love between Michelle and me. Even before she could talk, she would squeal with delight and hold out her little brown arms to me when I would enter a room.

Michelle's enthusiastic greetings resulted in one of my greatest moments of embarrassment. For some reason during these early years, Michelle dubbed me "Aunt Pattiwhacker." Where she came up with this charming extension to my name, I have no idea.

One Christmas Eve, I walked ceremoniously onto the platform of Westminster Christian Center with the church choir to present the annual holiday program. The auditorium was filled with people. Tall, flickering red candles and soft Christmas music set a beautiful mood for worship.

As I solemnly led the choir procession, the quiet dignity of the moment was shattered. From the back of the auditorium came a shriek: "HI, AUNT PATTIWHACKER!"

Her yelling came in handy one day at the Japanese Deer Farm. As we walked through the enclosure petting the deer, I heard a familiar alarm sounding behind me.

"AUNT PATTIWHACKER! Help!"

A deer had swallowed the end of one of Michelle's hair ribbons and he was chewing his way down the ribbon towards her long, black pony tail.

An extended scuffle evolved between the deer, Michelle, and me as I struggled to pull the ribbon back out of the deer's mouth. With Michelle howling and the deer stoutly bracing four hooves embedded in the ground, another solution soon became more logical. I untied the other end of the ribbon from Michelle's pony tail and we watched as the deer finished his unusual midday meal.

From early childhood, Michelle had a God-consciousness in her spirit. We could always talk about spiritual things, and at an early age during a children's crusade she committed her life to the Lord Jesus Christ as her Savior.

I was speaking at a youth conference in Riverside, California, and had taken Michelle along with me. She was around four years old at the time and as we went for a walk through the hills surrounding the camp grounds, her short toddler legs had difficulty in keeping up with my longer gait.

Suddenly I realized I did not hear the rapid shuffle of Michelle's little feet behind me, and I turned around to see where she was.

Way down the slope of the hill I caught sight of her, squatting down and intently staring at the ground. She was so engrossed, she did not even answer when I called.

I walked back to find her looking at a large ant hill, the fragile walls of which had collapsed with big red ants running in all directions.

"Michelle, what are you doing? Come on! Hurry up," I said impatiently.

She looked up with wide, dark eyes and answered, "Aunt Patti, I'm busy here watching God's little creatures."

During these precious years, I too was watching a beautiful creation of His hands called Michelle, one of God's very special little creatures.

THE AUTHOR AND MICHELLE
Dedication Day

THE FLOWER GIRL

The Flower Girl

My sister Cathy struggled to achieve the maturity that having a child forced on her so early in life. Cathy was very intelligent and had no difficulty in obtaining work, but she was so young and there were many temptations in the popular lifestyles of young people in the 1970s.

But from the depths of her confusion, the early training of our Grandmother finally resurfaced and Cathy rededicated her life to the Lord. Shortly afterwards she met Lou Thomas, a fine Christian young man, who asked her to marry him. Lou was Italian and had four brothers and one sister.

Michelle's extended family grew as she endeared herself to her new grandparents, Grandma and Grandpa Thomas, and her new aunts and uncles. With her dark skin and eyes, Michelle looked more like her Italian step-father than she did her fair-skinned mother.

After their marriage, Cathy and Lou decided to move to the Midwest. The separation from Michelle was traumatic for me. I was still unmarried at the time, and Michelle filled a great void in my lonely single life. She was like a daughter to me and I felt the pain of this first separation deeply. At that time I wrote a bit of free verse, which years later I was to wonder if was prophetic:

Michelle
I remember...
Warm brown arms around my neck,
A sunny smile,
A special name upon sweet cherub lips,
Short toddler legs moving rapidly towards life...
And then, there was silence.

Michelle soon welcomed a sister to the family as Cathy and Lou had their first child. Keren was a mixture of both mother and father with Cathy's eyes and fair skin and physical features like her father. A dark-haired, brown-eyed brother followed a few years later when Jeremy joined the family circle.

Each summer, Michelle came to visit her Grandma and me. She would also spend time with Aunt Janet and Grandma Jessie. Late one warm summer evening, Michelle and I had gone to bed, sharing the double bed in my one bedroom apartment. I was exhausted from our day at Knott's Berry Farm, the swim in the pool, and the baking of chocolate-chip cookies. Michelle, however, was still a bundle of energy.

As we laid in bed, Michelle talked non-stop for two hours sharing what seemed to be every detail of her life since we had been together the previous summer. I drifted in and out of sleep, occasionally punctuating her conversation with "Oh really?...Uh-huh...Is that so?"

Finally there came a pause in the chatter. Michelle yawned and said, "Aunt Patti, I'm sorry. You are just going to have to stop talking now because I am tired and I want to go to sleep!"

The summer of 1976 was a special time. On June 19th I was to be married to Argis Daniel Hulsey, a wonderful Christian man the Lord had brought into my life. Cathy and Michelle both came to California for the occasion.

Michelle was the flower girl for our wedding. She wore a long, ruffled gown of pale green eyelet which was offset with kelly green trim. Carefully balancing her basket of flowers, Michelle preceded me down the aisle to the altar of Garden Grove First Assembly of God Church.

Just ten years later, this same little flower girl would walk before me through another corridor of life. She would once again precede me to the place of the marriage ceremony as part of the Bride of Christ.

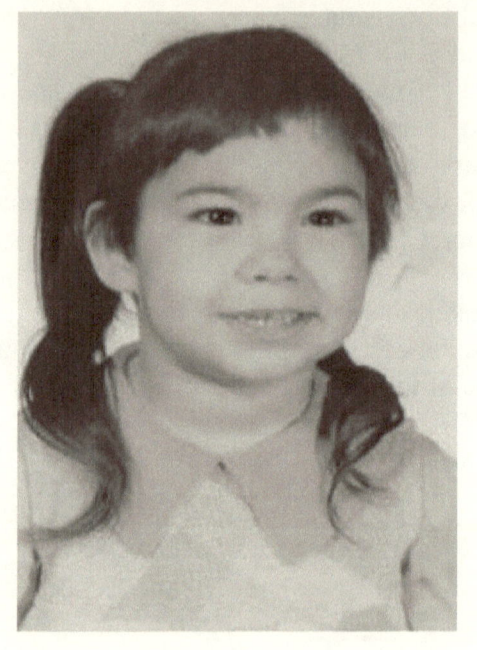

Buddy Purple Blossoms

At 15, Michelle was tall and slim with the fullness of womanhood touching her young figure. She was no longer a little girl. Only the long black hair and the flashing, mischievous dark eyes were the same.

That summer Michelle, Mom, and I went on a cruise up the inside passage to Alaska. Mom had been a long-time employee at K.D. Miller Electric Company in Whittier, and her boss was a real fan of Michelle. He helped plan the cruise and said he would send a car to take us to the airport.

Imagine our surprise when a shiny white stretch-limo pulled up in the driveway to take us to Los Angeles International Airport. The chauffeur held the door open for Michelle. Her dark eyes were shining with excitement as she exclaimed over and over, "Wow...the kids at home will never believe this!"

We flew from Los Angeles to Vancouver from where the S.S. Rhapsody departed. We sailed northward with port stops at Ketchikan, Sitka, and Juneau and a climaxing tour of Glacier Bay, Alaska.

Michelle had developed a wonderful capacity for making friends. She knew no stranger and endeared herself to people almost immediately. In a few days, she knew almost everyone on board and had explored every corner of the ship, including going up to the bridge and asking the captain for a personal tour.

These were days for making memories--ship-board exercise class, life-boat drill, exploring the Alaskan native craft shops, watching the salmon swim upstream, and wandering through the cool depths of the rain forest.

The summer of her 16th year, my husband and I were living in Madera, a small town in the heart of the agricultural community of Central California. Michelle enjoyed our new swimming pool and worked long hours with her Uncle Argis to help landscape our large front yard.

The following summer, when she was 17, Michelle returned to Madera to see the result of her efforts. The large dirt pile in which she had worked had been transformed into a beautiful green expanse of lawn bordered by neat rows of brick and colorful flowers. She especially enjoyed the garden--complete with a scarecrow--which we had planted in back of the house.

That summer I took Michelle to the nearby city of Fresno to see Valerie Howe, the minister who 17 years before had dedicated her to the Lord. While we visited together, Valerie taught Michelle how to crochet.

Michelle never believed in small beginnings. "I'm making you an afghan, Aunt Patti," she said ambitiously, her dark head bent over a hopeless tangle of yarn.

"Well, just be sure that I am not too old to enjoy it by the time you get it finished," I quipped.

Another summer of making memories like eating Bavarian cream-filled doughnuts--her favorite, walking through the Fresno Zoo, and munching tacos in Courthouse Park.

Michelle visited with Aunt Janet and Grandma Jessie that summer also. Aunt Janet had married and had her first son, Matthew, despite negative predictions by doctors that she could not have a child. Michelle immediately fell in love with Matthew and enjoyed mothering him during her brief stay.

This was a special summer. It was the summer before her final year at Portales High, a school in the New Mexico community of Portales where Cathy and Lou had settled. She was to return there for the 1985-1986 school term of her senior year.

All Michelle could talk about that summer was graduating with her friends and the hope that she could be in the school Maypole, an end-of-school celebration of spring. Only a few students were chosen from the senior class to be part of this special event, and she was hoping to be one of them.

We talked much that summer about her future. She wanted to go on to college and hoped to become a teacher. Her grades were good, and she had already worked some as a teacher's aide. She was deepening in her experience with the Lord. She told me about a special young man she liked, named Seth. A bright future was ahead, and we talked, planned, and dreamed together.

Late that summer, I took Michelle shopping for clothes for her senior year. We matched up quite an assortment of skirts, blouses, pants, and jackets. We coordinated the colors so she could mix and match outfits, then we made a list of the combinations so she could remember how things went together.

When my Mom came home from work, Michelle modeled all her new clothes in their various combinations. We topped the day off with a barbecue, during which Michelle cremated the spareribs and had smoke billowing all over the neighborhood. Then came the traditional baking of chocolate-chip cookies.

Michelle had planted some flowers called "Buddy Purples" in Mom's garden earlier that summer. From childhood, purple had been Michelle's favorite color. She kept a daily vigil over the plants until the flowers bloomed. That night she proudly showed off her Buddy Purple blossoms to me.

The next morning I left to return home. Michelle was to leave a few days later for Portales. We stood by Mom's front door.

"Have a great senior year baby, and I will see you next spring for graduation," I said as I hugged her goodbye. "I love you!"

"I love you too, Aunt Patti. I'll see you in the spring."

We waved goodbye, and I drove away. A simple parting, much like those of previous summers. The end of summer--and Michelle went back home to Portales and the Buddy Purple blossoms in the garden faded.

Days Of Destiny

When Michelle returned home, something happened which shattered her dreams. Lou and Cathy decided to move to El Paso, Texas, which meant Michelle could not complete her senior year at Portales High School.

After many tears over the big disappointment, Michelle entered the first semester of her senior year in El Paso. She made friends easily, kept up her grades, and participated in choir and dramatic productions. But she never lost the dream of graduating with her friends in Portales.

After she was 18 years of age in February, Michelle persuaded her Mom to let her go back to Portales for the spring semester. Michelle's Grandma and Grandpa Thomas owned a mobile home park, and Michelle could live in one of the small trailers on the grounds. She would be just a short distance from one of Lou's brothers and his wife who lived in the same park.

Spring semester at Portales High School found Michelle back with her friends. She was active in choir and helped one of her aunts in a ceramic shop.

When she returned to Portales, Michelle renewed her relationship with Seth, the young man of whom she had spoken fondly the previous summer.

Seth was one year older than Michelle and attended Eastern New Mexico University in Portales. He served as a security guard on campus and was enlisted in the National Guard.

Seth had experienced four different fathers during his brief life. His biological father deserted him when he was four years old. One stepfather badly abused him. At age 16, he was placed in a Christian children's home where he spent the rest of his young life until he was old enough to be on his own.

Seth first noticed Michelle as she waited at the school bus stop. They rode the same bus together and began to get acquainted. His quiet and shy nature was the opposite of Michelle's friendlier, outgoing traits, so their personalities balanced each other well.

Michelle had once written of love:

> *Love for a man is like a clown, for a clown is a man. A man that hides behind his makeup. His true identity is hidden from the world.*
>
> *A clown can change the mood in a room, by simply changing a little makeup. From up to down. A smile is happy, a frown is sad. Only two feelings are possible.*
>
> *Men hide from emotions and put up a front. Most of the feelings they show are fake and untrue. They say things they don't mean. It is the only way they know.*
>
> *But don't give up. There are some men that have come out. No kidding, no false lines, but true feelings.*
>
> *As for me, I have heard of such men. I thought a few times that I found one. But I found out there was only makeup.*

In Seth, Michelle believed she had found a relationship without the "makeup." She wrote of her feelings for him:

> *Times have changed...*
> *My heart has changed.*
> *My heart has feeling...*
> *I have fallen in love.*
>
> *A few times before I thought I had love.*
> *Now I know I only had care.*
>
> *...Love is wonderful, now I know...*
> *Full of smiles and secrets just between us.*
> *To have fun just being together.*

And Seth wrote fondly of Michelle:

> *My Michelle*
>
> *Loving, caring and warm black hair,*
> *brown eyes and shorter than I.*
> *Understanding, even in unpredictable situations.*
>
> *Others may not say she's cute, but I do,*
> *because beauty is only skin deep.*
> *The main thing, no matter what, I love her.*

During spring vacation, Michelle and Seth were engaged. They planned a summer wedding and wanted to attend Eastern New Mexico University together the following year. Michelle had already been accepted at the school and received a partial scholarship in the department of education.

A wedding date was set for shortly after graduation, and Michelle selected peach and apricot for her wedding colors. I bought her a wedding guest book in these shades, and she planned to wear my wedding veil with a special dress she had selected. Because Lou was away on military duty, she asked my husband, Argis, to give her away.

One month before May 22, Michelle wrote Aunt Janet describing details of her new life on her own:

> *Seth is a Christian and we believe the same. He comes over every day except Monday and Thursday, because he works on these days.*
>
> *We watch television and he works outside in the garden and lawn...We have set the wedding date for July 3rd...I will have to get the gears in motion for it in a few weeks.*

In a P.S. on the letter, she added:

> *Sorry I was so sloppy. I had to hurry to get this done.*

She did not realize how true this statement was. With each passing day, she was rapidly running out of time.

It was in this letter that Michelle spoke of those who had such a great influence in her life..."my grandmother, Jerry, Aunt Patti, Aunt Janet, Grandma Jesse" who made her "the most cared for little girl in the world."

How precious these words would become one short month later.

In late spring, I went to visit Mom and we planned the trips for Michelle's forthcoming graduation and wedding. Mom bought new luggage and we booked our flight tickets.

For Michelle's wedding we selected a dress for Mom in soft shades of peach--which was Michelle's wedding color--and purple, which was her favorite color.

While in town, I visited with Aunt Janet, who was also making plans to go to Michelle's wedding. As we parted, I said words which were to haunt us both a few weeks later.

"Well Janet, I will see you at the funeral if not before." I immediately caught my error...

"Funeral? What am I saying? I mean I will see you at the wedding!"

Janet laughed. "I was wondering," she said. "Marriage isn't that bad!"

Words of destiny, days of destiny that moved us toward the final days.

ALASKAN CRUISE
AGE 15

The Final Days

Graduation was to be on Memorial Day which fell that year on May 26. I spoke with Michelle a few days before.

"I got my senior pictures, Aunt Patti," she said.

"Great! When do I get one?," I asked.

"Well, I'm so busy I don't know if I will have time to get them in the mail," she answered. "I'll just bring them with me when I come out to California, okay?"

We discussed a recent letter I had written to her in which I expressed concern over some areas in her life, including her marriage at such a young age and her personal relationship with the Lord.

Michelle expressed sincere love for Seth and assured me that he was a true Christian. She also shared her desire to set every area of her life right with the Lord.

As we finished the conversation I said, "Michelle, I love you..."

"I love you too, Aunt Patti." They were the last words I would ever hear from her lips.

Wednesday, May 21, Michelle talked by phone with her Mom in El Paso. Cathy had plans to leave El Paso for Portales on Saturday, May 24, coming in a few days early for the graduation.

Michelle's conversation that Wednesday evening was bright and bubbly, excited about her plans for the next few days. She had realized her dream and been selected to participate in the school spring Maypole. She chatted excitedly about the forthcoming event.

Michelle made a list of the important things she needed to do Thursday...

> *Thursday, May 22nd:*
> *-Graduation rehearsal.*
> *-Tests.*
> *-Call ACT.*
> *-Take blue dress to Grandma to hem.*
> *-Maypole dress rehearsal: 7:00 p.m.*

Michelle went to graduation rehearsal and took her final tests Thursday morning. That afternoon, she called the ACT offices regarding her college entrance examinations.

But she never completed this list. She never made it to the Maypole rehearsal. She had made other lists of things to do for Friday through the following Monday. The final event on the list was for Monday, May 26. It was "graduation."

But her "graduation" came early.

The Longest Night

"Seth has shot Michelle."

The four words echoed like a scream through the corridors of my mind as I hung up the telephone from my initial call to Portales Hospital.

"They are trying to stabilize her," I told Argis. "Grandma Thomas says it looks bad."

After I dialed Mom and gave her the news, Argis and I went to prayer. We prayed the doctors would be able to stabilize her quickly and get her into surgery. We prayed God would guide their hands as they ministered life to her body.

We thanked God for the miracle we expected. Both of us had been vitally involved in Christian ministry and had witnessed many such miraculous interventions by God. One of our dear friends, given only six months to live by doctors, had been healed of incurable cancer. On one occasion, I had my hands on the ears of a nine-year-old deaf girl when God healed her. We had seen cripples rise from wheelchairs to walk, healed by the power of God. We prayed intensely, with faith, believing for victory for Michelle. We knew we would witness a great miracle in the next few hours.

In the hospital in Portales, a battle between life and death was ensuing in the emergency room. Michelle had been brought by ambulance to the hospital in a special pressurized body bag to try to stabilize her blood pressure and reduce shock. A team of eight doctors labored over her.

"I need an IV started here! Remove the bag...careful!"

"Prepare an OR room..."

"Blood pressure is falling, doctor..."

"Michelle, Michelle....can you hear me?"

"I need x-rays on this right side, STAT..."

"Have the crash cart standing by!"

"I need a blood type, cross and match."

In the midst of the confusion of activity, Michelle called out for Seth, but he was not there. Back at Michelle's trailer another tragic scene was being enacted. Seth was being taken into custody by the police...

> *"You have the right to remain silent. If you give up that right to remain silent, anything you say can and will be used against you in a court of law. You have the right to an attorney and to have that attorney present with you during questioning..."*

And on the road from El Paso to Portales as Cathy drove furiously to try to get to Michelle, yet another drama unfolded. A few miles out of White's City, New Mexico, her car broke down.

She got out of the car and lifted the hood. Already stunned by the tragic phone call and the urgency of her mission, her mind was paralyzed. She couldn't decide what to do next.

State Trooper Officer Michael Hickey was on routine patrol when he received the call of the disabled vehicle and the details of Cathy's urgent mission. He came to their assistance, put Cathy, Keren, and Jeremy in the back seat of the patrol car, turned on the red light and siren, and they were on the road again.

When Officer Hickey reached the end of his geographic jurisdiction, another patrol car waited and Cathy and her children were transferred to it. The transfer continued from car to car, as the entire state trooper force between White's City and Portales was mobilized to get Cathy to Michelle's side.

As the patrol car sirens screamed into the darkness of night carrying Cathy and the children northward, another state trooper's car was speeding from Portales to Roswell, New Mexico. The doctors had stabilized Michelle and were going to take her into surgery, but they were low on supplies of her blood type in the small Portales blood bank.

Deputy Charles Vannatta of the Sheriff's Department in Portales was dispatched from Portales to Roswell to obtain additional units from their larger blood bank. He made the 90 mile trip in 20 minutes in a desperate attempt to save the life of the young, dark-haired girl in the emergency room.

In Madera, California, my telephone rang again. It was Grandma Thomas.

"They have stabilized Michelle and taken her into surgery," she reported. "Keep praying. The doctors still say it doesn't look good."

I replaced the telephone receiver and started some coffee. The night would undoubtedly be a long one. I watched the dark liquid drip slowly through the filter into the pot. Was Michelle's life slipping just as surely from us?

No, I totally refused that negative thought and bolstered my faith. We had prayed. All we had to do was trust and wait for the miracle.

I reached for my Bible and opened it on the breakfast bar in front of me. The words leaped from the page:

> *God is our refuge and strength. A very present help in trouble. (Psalms 46:1)*

"Refuge" in Hebrew means "high place." The word "present" in Old English at the time of the King James translation meant "prompt in emergency, at hand, standing by in an emergency."

An assurance flooded my shock-shattered spirit. God was present, even in this dark hour. He was at hand, prompt to respond in emergency. He was the spiritual high place to which we could flee.

The telephone rang again. It was Grandma Thomas.

"Patti, the nurse just came out. Michelle is still in surgery. They said the bullet was a hollow point magnum and literally exploded inside her. It glanced off her spine and punctured vital organs. There is a hole in her diaphragm the size of a silver dollar and her liver is perforated. They are running out of blood plasma and are dispatching the deputy again to Roswell.

"And Patti...they said she might not make it..." she finished, trailing the last sentence without further comment or conclusion.

Deputy Vannatta's car shrieked through the darkness again from Portales to Roswell to secure the life-giving substance. Before the evening was over, Michelle would need 24 pints of blood plasma.

I replaced the telephone receiver and continued in prayer and in reading Psalms 46:

> *Therefore will not we fear, even though the earth be removed, and though the mountains be carried into the midst of the sea...*

Right now, our world was being shaken. We were being hurtled through circumstances in the middle of an unknown sea...

> *Though the waters roar and be troubled, though the mountains shake with the swelling.*

The waters--troubled, bitter waters of life--swirled around us...

> *There is a river, whose streams shall make glad the city of God, the holy place of the tabernacles of the Most High. God is in the midst of her; she shall not be moved: God shall help her, just after the break of dawn...*

Suddenly, in the midst of the passage, the Spirit of God spoke to my spirit...

"Release Michelle to Me."

"I have already done that," I answered silently. "The doctors have not given much hope. I have released her to You for a miracle."

"Release her to Me for a higher purpose", the voice spoke again to my spirit.

"Lord, I release Michelle to You. I release Michelle to Your purposes." I lifted my hands and whispered the words.

The sound of the telephone pierced the night again. I lifted the receiver. This time it was Grandpa Thomas. The nightmare of this evening had started with four words: "Seth has shot Michelle." It ended with four more words...

"She didn't make it."

Michelle had died on the operating table shortly before midnight.

A team of eight doctors and nurses had struggled to save her. One of the doctors had previously served with her step-father, Lou, in Vietnam. When Michelle died, he broke down and cried. "There was just too much damage. I simply could not save her."

Despite the efforts of the state troopers, Cathy had never reached Michelle. She received news of her death while being transferred from car to car en-route to Portales.

The patrol cars continued to bear Cathy northward, this time without red light and siren. There was no more urgency. It was too late. Michelle died alone, without the comfort of family and friends. Yet no one truly dies alone. The Good Shepherd is there to guide us through the valley of the shadow of death (Psalm 23).

As my sister traveled, I waited through the dark night for her to call upon arrival at Portales. I had experienced other long nights before...

> ...the long night of a bloody coup in Kenya where our evangelistic team was ministering.

...the long hours of arrest by the Communists in Nicaragua as we tried to enter the nation to conduct a Gospel crusade.

...Long nights of travel for the ministry, lonely nights in hotel rooms.

...but never was there a night as long as this one. Would this night never end?

...The day is Yours, the night also is Yours...
(Psalms 74:16)

Exhausted, I laid down on the couch in our family room which overlooked our spacious backyard. Moonlight reflected off of the still waters of the swimming pool.

...Though its waters roar and be troubled, we will not we fear...

In Portales, Cathy opened the door to a quiet hospital room still cluttered with life-saving equipment which now stood idle. There, with dark hair matted with blood and medical tubes still connected, was the body of her child.

The longest night was over...

...And there shall be no night there. (Revelation 22:5)

HIGH SCHOOL SENIOR
MICHELLE
The Name Means "Godly Woman"
"The Lord hath set apart the Godly for Himself."
(Psalm 4:3)

51

A Search For Meaning

The day which followed that longest night was one filled with no less emotion.

It was Maypole day at Portales High School, but the joy of the event was overshadowed by the news of Michelle's death. Michelle was known to everyone in the senior class and had many friends in the other grades. The entire school was shattered by the tragedy.

Michelle's friends in the vocal ensemble were most conscious of her vacant place as they sang at Maypole that evening. The Maypole was a celebration of life and spring, yet death stood silently among them.

Ironically, on that day the local newspaper carried the photos of members of the 1986 graduating class. Michelle was among them. But on the front page of the same paper was news of the shooting. On page two was her obituary.

We decided to have a memorial service for Michelle in Portales and an interment service in California to accommodate friends and relatives in both locations.

Cathy spent the day after the shooting making arrangements for the Portales service and the subsequent travel westward. Mom made arrangements in Whittier, California, for a graveside service and interment. I was left alone with my grief other than brief, emotion-laden calls updating me on the plans for both memorial services.

The police were investigating the circumstances of the shooting. They had released no factual reports as yet. We had only heard that Seth had been released to the custody of his former house-parents from the Christian children's home.

The blackberry vines in the field behind our house were at their peak of bearing. For want of something to do to keep me occupied, I headed out to the garden to pick berries.

As I began to pick I also began to pray. Soon all my hostility, anger, denial, and grief began to pour out before the Lord. From childhood, I had been taught to believe in the miraculous. I knew God performed miracles and I had witnessed great healings. But there had been no miracle for Michelle.

Perhaps I had not prayed hard enough. Or perhaps it was lack of faith on my part. Did not Jesus say, *"All things are possible to him that believeth"* and *"if you ask anything in my name it shall be done?"*

Failure never rested in God's promises, that I knew. Obviously, the failure must be mine. Guilt began to flood my soul. I cried until there were no more tears. Berry juice stained my hands and smeared my face where I wiped at the flood of tears.

I cried for my sister, performing her sad duties in Portales. I cried for my Mother accomplishing similar tasks in Whittier. The tears flowed for Michelle's high school friends, who instead of focusing on graduation and the joy of their lives ahead were rudely confronted with death.

I wept for Michelle, for the students she would never have the opportunity to teach, for the babies she would never bear, for all she could have been and done in life.

I cried for her real father, a father somewhere who didn't even know that his daughter had died.

Then came the questions. "Why?" is the most normal response in times of trouble. I had encountered the question many times before in counseling others...

-Why did God let my child die?
-Why did my husband desert me?
-Why do I have this terrible disease?
-Why did I lose all I possessed?
-Why, why, why?

And I thought I had comforted these people. I had given neat little answers to the complex question of "why." Tidy theology, neatly packaged, delivered from study and observation, but not from personal experience.

But none of these standard prepackaged answers worked for me now. None of the "God knows best" or "all things work together for good." In my thinking, things hadn't worked together for good. There had been no miracle. Michelle was dead.

At least most of those I had counseled had only to deal with "Why?" There was another pressing question in this situation. That question was "What?" What happened in that little trailer that resulted in Michelle's death? What was a gun doing there in the first place? And what on earth caused Seth to shoot Michelle?

Suddenly I realized my hands were bleeding where I had heedlessly scratched them reaching underneath vines for the berries. As I watched the blood trickle, my heart cried out, "Where was God when Michelle's blood was spilling out on the floor of that little trailer house, when her side was pierced by that bullet?"

Then, suddenly I knew the answer. God had looked on as the side of His own Son was pierced and His blood spilled upon the ground. But there had been meaning and purpose in that death for the sins of the world. I could see no meaning in Michelle's death. It appeared senseless and without purpose.

As I continued to pick berries, I began to realize that the biggest, juiciest ones were hidden beneath the tangled vines. In order to reach the best fruit I had to reach through the thorns. My hands were getting deep scratches.

As I realized this, the Lord spoke to my anguished soul and drew an analogy in the spirit world:

> *Sometimes that which is best and most beautiful is hidden from view and only obtained by the way of the thorns.*

My mind leaped to an immediate conclusion. That was it! There was some great purpose to all of this. We would discover the answers to our questions and from our understanding would come forth beauty.

I remembered my prayer when I first held Michelle in my arms, that if there was a purpose for me in her life that God would forge a special bond of love between us.

The special love had been there. Yet, although I influenced her some in life, I had seen no great purpose forged by our relationship. So somehow I must find purpose in her death.

The Bible says *"To everything there is a season, and a time for every matter or purpose under heaven...There is a time to be born, a time to die...A time to mourn...And in due season God will judge everything man does, both good and bad"*
(Portions of Ecclesiastes 3).

Surely we would find the answers. And of course, God would judge Seth for his actions. Maybe Michelle had decided to break off the relationship and Seth had tried to commit suicide. Most likely, Michelle gave her life trying to prevent Seth from taking his. Yes, I thought, that would give her death meaning and purpose.

Or--terrible though the thought was--if Seth had murdered her, this would surely come out in the investigation and justice would be done. That would certainly demonstrate that good triumphs over evil.

I examined alternatives and tried to squeeze meaning from each possibility, much as one squeezes the last drop from the mangled pulp of fruit. My thoughts were much like the tangled confusion of berry vines amidst which I worked.

I was familiar with the quest of such men as Viktor Frankl, survivor of the Nazi concentration camp, and his search for meaning in suffering. Frankl came to believe that each situation of suffering is unique, and that there is only one right answer to the question of "why?" He concluded that life ultimately means taking the responsibility to find the right answer.

There had to be meaning in Michelle's death. There simply must be purpose. I had to know. There was an answer, and I had to find it. I would take the responsibility to find it, and when I did, then the fact that God allowed her to die would be justified. I thought I could validate and vindicate the loss of Michelle as I discovered purpose and meaning in the tragedy.

That day in the berry patch, I began a search for meaning, but it was not to lead where I expected. I was seeking answers. I had not grasped the true meaning of the revelation that I had received regarding hidden beauty by way of the thorns.

Graduation Day

Graduation day for Portales High School was Monday, May 26. As the class marched in to the traditional music, there was a vacant spot left in the place where Michelle was to have been in the line.

"I want to graduate with my friends." The words reechoed in my heart. And her desire was granted, for Michelle's true graduation ceremony was held the following day. All her friends were there. The overflow section of the small funeral chapel had to be opened. The building was packed with friends, relatives, teachers, and classmates.

Even the sheriff who made the emergency trips for blood plasma came to honor the young girl he encountered so briefly in life. Several of the hospital staff who labored so fervently to save her were also present. There were so few to welcome Michelle in birth. There were so many gathered to bid her farewell in death.

Since Michelle's favorite color was purple, Cathy selected a casket of a light shade of amethyst and the same color predominated many of the flower arrangements which banked the altar.

Michelle wore a light tan dress trimmed in lace, a dress she had worn joyously in life to a formal dinner on our Alaskan cruise.

When Cathy and Lou entered the chapel, attention was riveted to the special section for family seating. There, entering with them and to be seated among them, was Seth.

In the few days since the shooting, response of the people of Portales had been divided over the young man. The facts of the investigation were not yet released. Some people were angry at him, while others viewed him with compassion. Others waited to voice their feelings until the facts of the shooting were released.

But one question occupied everyone's minds at this moment. What on earth was Seth doing sitting with the family of the very girl for whose death he was responsible?

On the Sunday between Michelle's death on Thursday and her funeral Tuesday, Cathy and Lou had gone to church services. The minister preached about a New Testament believer named Barnabas who helped Saul (Paul) when others would have nothing to do with him because of his past record of persecuting the church (Acts 9:26-27). Barnabas also stood by John Mark when Paul rejected him for service. Barnabas trained him until he was profitable for the work of God (Acts 15:36-40; 2 Timothy 4:11). The minister emphasized that if we do not express love and help those who are rejected, we may be aborting the future of a person who could become an Apostle Paul or a John Mark.

The investigation of Michelle's death was still underway. Seth had been advised not to talk to anyone concerning the details. The investigators would not release any information on the case. Still not knowing all the facts of the shooting, Lou and Cathy asked Seth to join the family for the funeral services in Portales.

Not all the family agreed with their decision and there was some contention over it. But had not Barnabas experienced similar difficulties with Paul when he made the decision to stand by John Mark?

So this was how Seth came to be present among those closest to Michelle as they entered the chapel that glorious spring afternoon.

When Rev. Sara Grill opened the memorial service, she read from the Scriptures as if to answer the unspoken questions raised by the congregation regarding Seth:

> *It is God that justifies...Who is he who condemns? It is Christ that died and furthermore is also risen, who is even at the right hand of God who also makes intercession for us. (Romans 8:33-34)*

The words clearly addressed the unspoken division over Seth. The answers were not all in yet, but regardless of the outcome God is the only one with the right to justify or condemn.

Then Rev. J.R. Camfield continued the Scripture reading:

> *Now He who has prepared us for this very thing is God...Therefore we are always confident, knowing that while we are at home in the body, we are absent from the Lord. For we walk by faith, not by sight...*
> *(Portions of 2 Corinthians 5:5-7)*

How true this verse was in that moment. We were groping blindly, walking by faith with limited understanding. He continued:

> *We are confident, I say, and willing rather to be absent from the body, and to be present with the Lord.*
> *(2 Corinthians 5:8)*

Was this true of Michelle? Was she really willing to die at such a young age, just when all of life was before her?

"The greatest event in a Christian's life is to be absent from the body and at home with Jesus Christ," said Rev. Camfield. "This is not a sad day, but a day of rejoicing. Michelle knew Jesus Christ. To those who know Jesus Christ, this is the true day of graduation. This is Michelle's graduation."

Then Carol Camfield stood to sing *"My Tribute: To God Be The Glory." [*]* Just ten years previously, the words to this melody had filled another chapel when Michelle had walked down the aisle as flower girl at my wedding.

> *How can I give thanks,*
> *for the things He has done for me,*
> *Things so undeserved,*
> *yet He gave to prove His love for me,*
> *The voices of a thousand angels,*
> *could not express my gratitude,*
> *All that I am and ever hope to be,*
> *I owe it all to thee...*

What a beautiful gift God had given to us in Michelle. There was no way to express our gratitude for her short life...

> *Oh let me live my life,*
> *and let it be pleasing Lord to thee,*
> *And should there be any praise,*
> *let it go to Calvary,*
> *With His blood He has saved us,*
> *with His power He has raised us,*
> *To God be the glory,*
> *for the things He has done.*

---

[*] *"To God Be The Glory," by Andre' Crouch.*

The last time I heard the words of this song, Michelle had been walking down a flower-strewn aisle to the altar on my wedding day. Now I pictured her passing through gates of pearl on streets of gold, walking right into the arms of her waiting Savior.

Rev. Hugh Wallis continued the Scripture reading:

> ...*For the Lord does not see as man sees; for man looks on the outward appearance, but the Lord looks at the heart.* (1 Samuel 16:7)

"Man has a tendency to look on the outward appearance, the way things appear to be," he said. "But things are not always as they appear to be."

Rev. Ron Sears read from Psalm 126:

> *When the Lord brought back the captivity of Zion,*
> *We were like those who dream.*
> *Then our mouth was filled with laughter,*
> *And our tongue with singing.*
> *Then they said among the nations,*
> *"The Lord has done great things for them."*
> *The Lord has done great things for us,*
> *And we are glad.*

How could Michelle's death be a great thing? How could our mouths ever be filled with singing and laughter again? Rev. Sears continued:

> *Those who sow in tears shall reap in joy. He who continually goes forth weeping, bearing seed for sowing,*

shall doubtless come again with rejoicing, bringing his sheaves with him.

How precisely the Lord led each of these ministers in the selection of the Scriptures. Each verse would unfold with new meaning in the events of the coming months.

Just before the message, a song was presented by the high school ensemble of which Michelle had been a member. Young voices lifted in *"A Parting Blessing"*:

> *May the road rise to meet you,*
> *May the wind be always at your back,*
> *May the sun shine warm upon your face,*
> *May the rain fall soft upon your field,*
> *And until we meet again,*
> *May God hold you in the palm of His hand.*

Somehow I believe Michelle joined in the chorus from another world where she was already being held in the palm of God's hand.

Rev. Randy Grill, who had known Michelle since early childhood, delivered the "graduation" message. He opened with the words of Jesus:

> *Jesus said to her, "I am the resurrection and the life. He who believes in Me, though he may die, he shall live. And whoever lives and believes in Me shall never die."*
> *(John 11:25-26)*

"These are strange words...`shall never die'," Rev. Grill said, "especially since we are here today because of death. But as we read the Scriptures, we find it speaks of death of only one group of people. Those who do not know Jesus Christ as their personal Savior.

"For those who believe, they go to be `with the Lord'. The word `death' is not used of a believer," he explained.

"When a man named Nicodemus asked Jesus how to inherit eternal life so he would not die, Jesus explained to him `You must be born again'. Jesus was speaking of a spiritual experience which comes through the forgiveness of sins (John 3).

"Jesus explained that when you are born again, there are evidences in your life, just as there are visible evidences when the wind blows.

"I have known Michelle since she was three years of age," recalled Rev. Grill. "She stayed in our home on many occasions. There were many evidences of a good confession and of good works and deeds.

"When we know Jesus Christ, as Michelle did, we have already passed from death unto life. When we close our eyes in what the world calls `death', we have only taken one last glimpse of this world and opened our eyes in the presence of our Savior (2 Corinthians 5:6-8).

"To the world it seems tragic that Michelle would come so soon to the end of a life which seemed so promising," commented Rev. Grill. "It seems tragic that a young graduating class would have this special time in their lives marred by the fact that one of their number has already come to the end of the road.

"But it is not tragic from God's perspective. He looked down and saw that Michelle had finished her earthly course. She was ready to graduate.

"When we graduate from high school, we hear many great words which challenge us to set goals for living. We have our dreams for life, but we often leave God out of our goals and our dreams. We prepare for life, but we do not prepare for death.

"There is no rehearsal for the day you die, such as you had for graduation. Michelle had no rehearsal, but she was ready. We must prepare now for that day when we, too, will face death.

"You are all here because Michelle touched your life in some way," continued Rev. Grill as he scanned the large crowd. "Do not ever give up on life just because of tragedy. There are many beautiful Michelles in life."

"When I was asking the Lord what I should say of Michelle's short life, the Lord gave me this verse:

> *You did not choose Me, but I chose you and appointed you that you should go and bear fruit, and that your fruit should remain... (John 15:16)*

"When Jesus spoke these words, He indicated that as believers our lives should have lasting meaning and purpose.

"As I reflected on this verse, I remembered that Michelle was loyal, understanding, and kind to people. She had her sweet ways. She ministered in church in song. What she had, she shared so freely. But what real fruit could I talk about in her short life? "Then God spoke to me," said Rev. Grill. "God said, 'This is Michelle's greatest hour. In this hour she is having the opportunity to speak to her family and friends'.

"The greatest spiritual fruit of Michelle's life will be borne in this hour if her friends and family who loved her so dearly will set their course towards God."

Another minister friend, Rev. Paul Roppe, concluded the service.

"Michelle knew what it was to present her body to Christ a living sacrifice," he said. "Today, God receives Michelle's sacrifice. God is the Author and Finisher of our faith. Michelle's faith is finished. In 18 short years, Christ has done the work in Michelle that was necessary in order to bring her before the throne of God."

Rev. Roppe closed in prayer. "We thank You for Michelle's radiant testimony and the example of what Jesus can do in the life of a young person in our midst."

Then Rev. Roppe spoke the words I had spoken just a few short days ago, during that longest night.

"...So Father, we release her. We release her to You. We say, 'Michelle, be gone, be with your Savior!'"

As the service concluded and the long line of friends and relatives filed past Michelle's casket, her harvest began to come in.

Michelle's best friend stood beside her casket and committed her life to Jesus Christ. Young person after young person made similar commitments. In Michelle's death, her friends found life. At last Seth stood beside the open casket. He softly touched Michelle's long black hair. Tears streamed down his face..."I'll meet you there, Michelle. I promise I will!"

As God promised, it was Michelle's greatest hour as she brought forth fruit that remains.

> *Verily, verily, I say unto you, Except a corn of wheat fall into the ground and die, it abideth alone: but if it die, it bringeth forth much fruit. (John 12:24)*

The Final Journey

With the spring had always come Michelle. From the time she was so young that she had to travel in custody of flight attendants, Michelle had come "home" to California in the spring. But this year, she would not come. How could the spring come without Michelle?

But Michelle *was* coming. This time, she was coming home to stay. Wednesday, May 28, 1986, she began her journey.

Cathy, Lou, Keren, and Jeremy boarded an airplane which would carry them westward from New Mexico to California. They struggled with emotion as they realized that deep in the recesses of the cargo-hold a casket was being loaded.

Michelle was making her final journey home. Michelle was already enjoying her new life in Heaven of course, but her earthly body was coming home to be interred beside the her great grandmother and great grandfather at Rose Hills Memorial Park. In reality, Michelle had already made her journey home. She was already home with Jesus.

As they traveled westward, Argis and I were traveling southward from Madera to Southern California. I too was struggling. I was remembering my journey through these hills a few short months previously. I had been going down south to help Michelle shop for school clothes...

"Goodbye, Aunt Patti. I'll see you in the spring."

And now, it was spring and I was going to see Michelle. The hills through which we traveled burst with new life. But the green meadows and wild flowers seemed bright and gaudy, taunting us with their joyous beauty. Surrounded by life, I saw only death.

When Argis and I arrived in Whittier, we went first to the Rose Hills Mortuary to view Michelle. When we entered the quiet chamber, I was engulfed with the odor of carnations and roses. I hesitated just inside the door, examining the cards on bouquets of flowers, trying to get a grip on my emotions for the viewing which would confirm a reality I had not really accepted.

Argis went directly to her. "She looks beautiful," he said. I blindly groped to his side and he took my hand. I wiped away the tears to clear my vision. Before me was the earthly shell of a beautiful young woman. Olive skin, thick dark hair falling across the satin pillow, and her eyes--they looked as if at any moment they would open, and we would see that dark, mischievous twinkle again. The features were all there, but it was not Michelle. There was no spirit of life. I knew when I looked at her that my true Michelle was gone.

Later that day just before the graveside service and interment, Mom, Cathy, and I returned to the slumber room. We had been the first three to greet Michelle when she entered the world just 18 short years before, the first to lay eyes upon her. It was fitting that we would be the last three to bid farewell to her beautiful earthly vessel.

Cathy had brought Michelle's graduation cap and gown from Portales. They had selected white for the graduating class of 1986. She placed them into the casket with Michelle. But Michelle had really already received her graduation robe:

...And to her was granted to be arrayed in fine linen, clean and white: for the fine linen is the righteousness of the saints. (Revelation 19:8)

Then Cathy tucked Michelle's high school diploma close to her side. "Here you are baby. You earned it," she said.

When Cathy gave me Michelle's senior class picture, Michelle's words echoed in my memory: "I may not have time to mail one to you. I'll bring it when I come."

The afternoon sunlight warmed the western slope of the hillside as we gathered for the final tribute to Michelle. When my eyes met those of Aunt Janet, I knew the same words echoed in her memory as they did in mine--that strange slip of words I had made just weeks before: "I'll see you at the funeral."

Argis conducted the brief interment service and he spoke final words of comfort:

"Michelle is not dead, but alive with Jesus. This is only the earthly house in which she lived, which we lay to rest today. Her soul has returned to God who gave it.

"We cannot change the past. We cannot change what has happened. Michelle cannot come to us, but we can go to her. The decisions we make now will affect whether or not we go to her."

The climaxing moment came as we bowed our heads in prayer and Argis said, "Lord, we give Michelle to You." My eyes focused on Mom as he said these words. She was wearing the dress she had planned to wear to Michelle's wedding.

Michelle had asked Argis to give her away at her wedding. Now he did just that. He gave her away to become part of that innumerable host of the Bride of Christ. Just as when she served in our wedding as flower girl, Michelle had preceded me down the aisle to the place of the marriage as part of the Bride of Christ.

Then we walked away, leaving a lonely flower-covered casket on the hillside, a bleak picture emblazoned forever in our memories, stark in contrast to the glory of the late afternoon sun.

Facing Bitter Waters

The most difficult time in any suffering is the time after the initial shock has worn off when, somehow, one must return to the everyday routine of living.

-When the vacant rooms taunt the truth of a husband who has deserted his family.

-When the reality of a terminal illness is confronted.

-When the urgent duties of an emergency have all been accomplished.

-When the last beautiful words are spoken over the departed loved one.

It is then that the reality of suffering--no matter what the loss --sets in.

We received an abundance of loving expressions from friends and members of the Portales community. The photographer who had taken Michelle's senior pictures wrote to express how *"the whole school felt this loss."*

Michelle's classmates poured by the mobile home where Cathy and Lou were staying temporarily in Portales to express their love.

The grandmother of two of Michelle's best friends said that although she never met Michelle, she had come to know and love her through her granddaughters.

The captain of the Police Department who was investigating Michelle's death summarized the feeling of the community:

> *Michelle's loss can never be replaced in the lives of her survivors. Everyone here connected with Michelle and the extensive efforts to save her life share in your bereavement.*
>
> *The loss of your loved one is shared by the community in which she lived and upon which she made such a positive impact. Each of us grieve in our own private way for such loss.*

Such expressions of comfort and love were helpful, but there are depths in suffering which cannot be shared with another human being.

Grief has been described as a process with different stages which vary with the type of loss involved and the culture and personality of the individual. It begins with the first awareness of loss and finally ends when you can remember the reality of what has happened without intense emotional pain.

Some have held grief to be unchristian, but the Bible says Jesus was a man acquainted with grief (Isaiah 53:3). The Bible indicates there is a time to mourn (Ecclesiastes 3:4), and those who mourn are blessed because they will be comforted (Matthew 5:4). Tears are not a lack of faith. Jesus wept at the graveside of Lazarus (John 11:35). Tears are precious to the Lord, so precious that He collects and preserves each tear we shed and records them in a book (Psalm 56:8).

Paul said that *"we sorrow not as those which have no hope"* (1 *Thessalonians 4:13).* He did not say we were not to sorrow, just that we are not hopeless in our grief. God also sets the limits to our grieving. As surely as there is a *"time to mourn,"* there is a time to rejoice again (Ecclesiastes 3:4). Jesus bore your grief, so you need not continue to bear it or linger excessively in stages of mourning.

The grief over Michelle's death came in waves like the sea. It would recede for awhile, only to crash again in new force upon the soul. Only if one has truly suffered can they identify with such engulfing emotions.

Sometimes moments of anguish would be triggered by simple things--seeing the color purple, hearing the name "Michelle" shouted by a youngster to his playmate, or spotting a dark-haired, brown-eyed little girl in a crowd of children.

And then there was so much left which testified of the unexpected interruption of Michelle's life. When she was shot, Michelle had been packing to go home with her mother after graduation. Grandma Thomas had to finish packing her things.

I opened a drawer and discovered one of her scarves knotted exactly as she wore it. Then there was the afghan she had started for me, which never got beyond a small uneven square...the fireworks she saved from last summer to shoot off this year...the pair of ceramic penguins she had been working on at her aunt's shop. They all were mute testimony of a life interrupted, ending unexpectedly when the sound of a bullet pierced the hours of that early spring evening.

Through days that seemed like months, we waited for the results of the investigation. The police captain wrote apologetically:

The investigation conducted concerning this matter has been scheduled by the Assistant District Attorney for Roosevelt County, New Mexico, to be presented to a Grand Jury for their consideration on June 10, 1986.
The individuals involved in the incident and its aftermath have been either invited, or ordered by subpoena, to appear before the Grand Jury to testify.

Because of the pending status of this matter before the court, I am not able at this time to discuss the details disclosed in the investigation with anyone not connected with the investigation.

Following the Grand Jury's considerations, and depending on their findings, I may then be free to advise you of the details you seek.

So I had to wait in my search for understanding and meaning which would justify what I thought were the actions of God.

The Sunday after Michelle's interment, Argis and I attended our local church fellowship in Madera. I cannot tell you the title or subject of the message preached by the visiting minister, but the verses he read in the course of the message greatly impacted my life.

The Scripture passage he selected was from an event which happened to the nation of Israel shortly after God had delivered them from Egyptian bondage:

So Moses brought Israel from the Red Sea, and they went out into the wilderness of Shur; and they went three days in the wilderness, and found no water. And when they came to Marah, they could not drink of the waters of Marah, for they were bitter; therefore the name of it was called

75

Marah. And the people murmured against Moses, saying, "What shall we drink?" And Moses cried unto the Lord; and the Lord showed him a tree, which when he had cast into the waters, the waters were made sweet; There He made for them a statute and an ordinance, and there He proved them. (Exodus 15:22-25)

To this passage Rev. Burke related the verses which spoke of Jesus:

There shall come forth a rod out from the stem of Jesse, and a branch shall grow out of his roots... (Isaiah 11:1)

When he read these passages, their connection literally thundered together in my mind with powerful spiritual impact. The first seed of what would become known as the *"Bitter Waters"* message was planted.

I realized that bitter waters are a symbol of the difficult circumstances we face in life. God does not permit bitter waters-- these tragic events--for us to drink of them. We are not to ingest the bitterness of life's tragedies into our spirit. It is at bitter waters that God proves us to see of what our profession of faith consists.

Our response to bitter waters--all the tragic, difficult experiences of life--should be to cast the spiritual branch of the Lord Jesus Christ into the waters. We must look at each difficult situation and see how Jesus can be manifested in it. Then, when we cast in the "Rod of the Branch of Jesse" the bitter waters will be made sweet, even as when Moses cast the branch into the poisoned waters of Mara.

Michelle's death had brought me to the bank of bitter waters. How would I react as God proved me there? Could I cast in the rod of the Lord Jesus Christ and see these bitter waters made sweet?

"But how can I do this?" I questioned as I pondered these verses. "What must I do in order to cast the Lord Jesus into this situation?"

That which God spoke to my spirit was a simple command, yet it was the most difficult thing I had ever done. He told me to show His love to Seth, Michelle's fiancé, even without knowing the facts of the shooting, and to start by writing to him expressing that love.

Suddenly I realized the minister was concluding his message and had asked the congregation to stand for the closing prayer. He hesitated before praying. "God has shown me there is someone here with a broken heart," he said. Before he could even finish the appeal, I stumbled over my husband's feet and into the aisle to move to the front of the church.

This man did not know me or have knowledge of the events which had happened in the last few days, but as I stood before him the Spirit of the Lord spoke to me through him:

> *"God may not answer all your questions, but fix yourself to that which you do know. Fix yourself on God and His Word. If He chooses to reveal the answers to you, He will do it at a time when it will not crush you."*

That afternoon I wrote to Seth. It was difficult to do without knowing the facts of the shooting. In the business world, I had been trained to act from a position of strength on the basis of facts. Now I wrote from my spirit, without benefit of the advantage which comes from knowledge of the truth.

Casting In The Branch

In Portales, Seth held a long white envelope in his hands, hesitating to open it, afraid to read the message it contained. Finally, he ripped open the letter and spread its contents on the desk before him.

Dear Seth:

I want to say at the outset that I hold no bitterness towards you nor blame you in any way for Michelle's death. I say that first, because I do not want you to be afraid of reading the contents of this letter. Michelle loved you and because of that, I love you.

Michelle was like my own daughter and, of course, her death came as quite a shock. The 18 years God gave her on this earth were intricately entwined with my own life.

I do not know if Michelle shared the last letter I wrote her or discussed our last phone call. I talked with her about making sure of the timing of her marriage to you. She was so very young, and although you seemed like a nice person from her description, I just wanted her to be sure.

All she told me about you impressed me--that you were in college, a member of the National Guard, and that you were going to pursue a police career.

I told Michelle that we would support her in whatever decision she made--whether to marry you now, break it off, or wait awhile--but we just wanted her to be happy and to have the blessing of God on her life.

Seth, I do not know what happened in those last few minutes of Michelle's life. I know that you cannot talk about it since the investigation has not concluded yet. I hope that when you are ready and you can do so, you will share it with me.

I do know that Michelle loved you. She was the most forgiving little girl in the world, and she certainly would not be angry at you if she had lived.

Regardless of how it happened, Michelle would want you to go on living. She was always so happy and full of life herself.

Michelle poured her love into you, and that makes her part of you. That means a part of Michelle will always be with you.

Seth, you can give the greatest meaning to Michelle's life and death by what you do with your own life. If you waste your life--if you let this destroy you or if you take your own life in despair--then it will be like another little part of Michelle dying all over again.

If you go on with God's help to make something of yourself, then it is as if a part of her becomes victorious with you over this tragedy.

Make your life count for twice as much, Seth. Live life to the fullest. Go on to do great things and it will be as if Michelle is alongside of you doing them also.

Michelle said you were a Christian. Since I do not know you well, I do not know about your relationship with the Lord. Growing up in church is not enough. You must come to know the Lord as your personal Savior. If you have never experienced this, then the greatest thing that could come from this tragedy is for you to find Jesus. That would mean that through her death, you would find true life.

Whether we live to be 18 or 80, life is so short compared to eternity. I know I will see Michelle again, and I will have all eternity to be with her. You can have that same assurance.

Seth, please write me even though it might be hard. I need to know about you--who you are, what you are feeling--and most of all, how I can help a special person that Michelle loved.

> *Love and prayers,*
> *Aunt Patti*

Seth folded the letter and wept. The branch of the Lord Jesus had been cast into the bitter waters.

When Answers Aren't Enough

I held in my shaking hands the letter for which I had long awaited, but which I fearfully hesitated to open. The return address was "Portales Police Department."

The Grand Jury had met and I was sure that the contents of this letter held the answers to our questions. Was I really ready to face the answers? Could I continue to "cast the branch" of the Lord Jesus into the bitter waters despite knowledge of the truth? Could we continue to reach out to Seth in love regardless of what we learned?

The words spoken by Rev. Burke came to my mind...

> *"God may not answer all your questions, but fix yourself to that which you do know. Fix yourself to God and His Word. If He chooses to reveal the answers to you, He will do it at a time when it will not crush you."*

I slit open the envelope and skipped the formal salutations of the letter. Then I read carefully as Captain Sheffer recounted the events of May 22.

In the morning, Michelle had attended school. Seniors were off in the afternoon. Michelle returned home between 12 and 12:30 p.m.

She and Seth spent the afternoon together at the trailer packing up Michelle's things so she would be ready to go home with her mother after graduation. They washed clothes, emptied drawers, and cleaned up the trailer. As they worked, they chatted about Michelle's upcoming school activities and preparations for graduation.

Seth took a loaded .22 magnum single action revolver from the drawer of a night stand. He had originally purchased the gun for Michelle's protection when she expressed fear at being alone in the trailer.

Being in the National Guard, Seth was trained in the use of firearms, but Michelle had never been around guns and was afraid of the weapon. Even on this day, as he removed it from the drawer she urged him to unload it and pack it away.

Captain Sheffer explained the fatal moments:

> *Seth unloaded the revolver, but only took out five of the six rounds of ammunition, mistakenly thinking he had removed all six. He did not check to see if the revolver was completely unloaded. Seth attempted to lower the hammer of the revolver. The hammer slid out from under his thumb and the revolver discharged. The bullet struck Michelle.*

For a few moments, Michelle did not realize she was struck by the bullet. She walked into the hall, then suddenly leaned against the wall and slid down it.

"You shot me," she said simply to Seth.

Then the nightmare began. In panic, Seth fled Michelle's trailer to seek help. He ran to the trailer nearby where Michelle's Uncle Joey lived.

"I shot Michelle, I shot Michelle..." he was screaming the words over and over hysterically.

Joey shouted to his wife to call emergency services and then he and Seth raced back to Michelle's trailer.

As Seth had exited the trailer, the front door had locked behind him. He and Joey had to break the door in to get to Michelle. Then the ambulance arrived, and the dramatic attempt to save her life was underway.

In her final moments, Michelle told rescue workers and hospital attendants that the shooting was an accident. She cried out for Seth several times at the hospital before going into surgery. But Seth was in custody of the Portales Police being booked for felony manslaughter.

After an investigation and consideration by the Grand Jury, the charge had been reduced to negligent use of a firearm for which Seth would be tried in court. Finally the District Attorney had approved the release of the information to the family.

I stared at the report in shock. It was an accident. It was a senseless, tragic accident.

If it had been murder, though no less tragic, one could perhaps accept it more easily since sinful men and their actions are part of our troubled world.

If Michelle had died trying to prevent a suicide attempt, her death would have been noble and with purpose.

I could even understand better if she had been killed by a drunk driver. Such accidents are, again, the results of sinful man in a troubled world.

And death by a natural causes? Scripture confirms we are living in mortal bodies subject to death and disease.

But why would God permit such a tragic accident? Why would God allow such a terrible thing to happen to two young people, both believers, who were doing their best to serve Him? They were clean-cut Christian kids--no drugs, no alcohol, no gangs.

I knew the Bible spoke clearly of the sovereignty of God. But if God was sovereign--in control of all things--then could He not have prevented this accident? Was the universe really out of control and man just a victim of fate? Were such accidents actually beyond His intervention? The answer to *what* had happened only generated new questions about *why*.

When Michelle's Grandma Jessie heard the results of the investigation, she went outside and paced angrily up and down the driveway. A long time later she came inside. "It isn't fair," she said. "Michelle came into the world through an accident, and she went out of the world by an accident."

Was that all Michelle's life was? One big accident?

One evening as I drove to the Bible school where I taught, I was struggling deep within. How could I challenge these young people when I had no answers for my own situation? I seriously considered turning the car around to go back home.

Instead, I switched on the radio to create a distraction from my tormenting thoughts. Suddenly, the peace of God filled the car as I heard these words:

> *You have faced the mountains of desperation,*
> *You have climbed you have fought you have won,*
> *But this valley that lies coldly before you,*

Casts a shadow you cannot overcome...

I clutched the steering wheel. That was exactly where I was. I had faced spiritual mountains before. I had fought and climbed and won. But never a challenge like this. The words continued:

> *And just when you thought you had it all together,*
> *You knew every verse to get you through,*
> *But this time the sorrow broke more*
> *than just your heart,*
> *And reciting all those verses just won't do...*

Then the chorus burst forth:

> *When answers aren't enough there is Jesus,*
> *He's more than just an answer to your prayer,*
> *Then your heart will find a safe and peaceful refuge,*
> *When answers aren't enough, He's there.*

I didn't have the answers, but I had the Answerer. I had Jesus. The words continued...

> *Instead of asking why did it happen,*
> *Think of where it could lead you from here*
> *And as your pain is slowly easin',*
> *You can find a greater reason,*
> *To live your life triumphant through the years.* [*]

I had been asking over and over again, "Why did it happen?" I was dwelling on the past. Never once had I focused on the future. Where could it lead from here?

------

[*] *"When Answers Aren't Enough."* From the album *"Somebody's Brother"* by Scott Wesley Brown, The Sparrow Corporation, 1985.

On June 23, 1986, Seth again appeared in court for preliminary examination on the reduced charge of negligent use of a firearm. Several subsequent hearings followed. With each court appearance, the nightmare went on. The details of the shooting were rehearsed repeatedly like a bad vinyl record stuck in a scratched groove. Finally on July 14, the waiting was over. Seth was given 18 months probation.

Shortly after the sentencing, Seth called me. For over an hour he poured out his heart. The terror of that night--the disbelief when they told him Michelle was dead, the guilt of responsibility he felt for her death, and how he felt as he stood beside her casket.

"I didn't have a chance to tell her goodbye. That was the hardest part," he said.

I understood, for I too had struggled with the same feelings. In anticipated death, there is comfort in those last moments recognized as the final hour--being able to say goodbye. In sudden death, there is no such comfort.

The day just before the shooting, Michelle had given Seth one of her senior class pictures. On the back she had written, *"With all my love...I will love you until the day I die."* The next day, she did.

Seth cried when the judge gave him word of the probation which would end his long ordeal. He wrote me later:

"...They were tears of happiness that it was all finally over.

I was like a track runner running hurdles. The hurdles were the problems I have been going through. I got over the first hurdles of blaming myself, not being able to get over her death, and just not believing she wasn't alive anymore.

After I got over these hurdles, I had this very big one to get over. With God's grace and all the prayers, I cleared it. God has become my coach, and He has shown me how to overcome these hurdles.

I know Michelle would be happy for me, because she wouldn't want anything to happen to me either. I'm still confused about things right now. I feel lost and out of place wondering what to do next.

There will never be anyone like Michelle. She will always be a part of me."

As we grieved together, our hearts were joined in even deeper love for this young man, rejected by his family, his life so tragically shattered.

Seth responded to our love. He told us that for the first time in his life, he felt as if he really had a family. He expressed his feelings in a letter to Cathy and Lou:

"You are a wonderful Christian family and had a wonderful daughter. Thank you for being there when I needed you. I could see God's love in Michelle's life and in yours. Thank you for your help through this. Without you and the Lord, it would be almost impossible."

By casting the "rod of the Branch of Jesse" into bitter waters we became Seth's family. He had planned to become part of the family through marriage, but we were forged together by a greater bond, that of human suffering. We had lost Michelle, but Seth had been substituted by God's grace.

A Time To Die

Perhaps the moment after ecstasy:
after feeling the full fierce, force of life;
after knowing love,
and while love is still warm...

Perhaps that is the time for dying;
before everything and
everyone has turned sour,
before life is a burden,
before the thrill of waking
to a new day is gone,
before we long for death.

To die while bursting with life
brimming with vitality,
longing to live...

Perhaps this is the time to die...[*]

---

[*] From the pages of the notebook of Darlene Bee, Wycliffe
Bible Translator who perished in an airplane crash on the mission
field. From "Into The Glory" by Jamie Buckingham, Logos
International.

The Bitter Waters Message

I was driving through the hills from Madera to Los Angeles again, the same route I traveled just three months previously. On that journey I had been going to face death at Michelle's final interment service. Now I traveled the same road to impart life. I was going to minister at a women's seminar at Arrowhead Springs, California.

Had it not been that I was scheduled for the meeting many months in advance and it had been widely advertised, I would not be making this journey. I would have canceled the meeting because I just did not feel emotionally ready for public ministry. Just as surely as the fading touches of green on the hills around me struggled for life in the hot August sun, I too was struggling.

In the months since Michelle's death, I had discovered the true meaning of "hidden beauty by way of the thorns." I had learned more about bitter waters as I searched for meaning in the suffering we had experienced. As a result of my desperate search, the *"Bitter Waters"* message had been birthed. Now God was speaking to me about sharing this message at the women's seminar, but I was struggling. I did not feel emotionally capable of doing this.

The building was packed with women that Saturday morning. As I entered the service, I carried with me two sets of notes. One set was for the *"Bitter Waters"* message. The other notes were for a different message which I felt more competent to deliver. I struggled with the decision.

After the opening worship, I was called to the platform and turned to face the group of women. My hands hesitated over the two sets of notes.

"This morning I would like to share with you from God's Word a message entitled... `Facing Bitter Waters.'"

There...I had said it. I felt a release in my spirit. Emotion was replaced by confidence in God's power to share this revelation. I felt His supernatural strength in my weakness as I began.

"When I speak of `bitter waters' I am using the term to refer to the difficult circumstances of life. Bitter waters are of varied types. They may be loss by death, violence, divorce, or accident. They may be bitter experiences of abuse or rejection. But the common factor is that they are all bitter circumstances of life.

"The text for this message is taken from an experience of the nation of Israel immediately after God had delivered them from Egyptian bondage:

> *So Moses brought Israel from the Red Sea, and they went out into the wilderness of Shur; and they went three days in the wilderness, and found no water. And when they came to Marah, they could not drink of the waters of Marah, for they were bitter; therefore the name of it was called Marah. And the people murmured against Moses, saying, What shall we drink? (Exodus 15:22-24)*

"There are two things common to all people of every nation. They are common factors no matter where we live, what color our skin, or what language we speak.

"The first is that sin is present in every society. The Bible clearly indicates that all men have sinned and are in need of a Savior (Romans 3:23).

"The second common factor is that all men everywhere experience suffering. We do not like to talk about suffering. We do not hear a great deal of preaching on this subject. We prefer to hear messages on victory and prosperity, and these things are good, as they are part of the revelation of God.

"But the Bible is not just a book of promises concerning the abundant life. It is a record of suffering, both of the righteous and the unrighteous. We avoid the subject of suffering because there are elements involved in it that we do not understand and cannot explain.

"When Jesus was here on earth and spoke of the suffering He was to face on the cross, many of His followers deserted Him (John 6:55-66). They expected the Messiah to reign in power and glory. Instead, He spoke of suffering. They could not understand, so they turned away.

"If you do not know how to deal with the bitter waters of life, you too may turn from following Jesus when you face suffering.

"Suffering originally entered the world through the sin of man (Genesis 3). There are different ways suffering enters our lives and there are different kinds of suffering, but all suffering is a result of Satan at work in the world today.

"God did not create suffering, but--as you will learn as we examine the subject of bitter waters--God can take that which is intended for evil and turn it for good to accomplish His purposes."

Experiencing Bitter Waters

"There are five main ways that bitter waters--difficult, tragic, and painful circumstances of life--may flow into your life. All suffering comes through one of these five channels:

"First, bitter waters result from your own sin. Jonah is an example of such suffering. In disobedience to God's instructions, Jonah headed the opposite direction from Ninevah where he had been commanded to go and preach repentance. He experienced a terrible storm at sea and ended up in the belly of a great fish because of his disobedience (Jonah 1-2). He is an example of what the prophet Jeremiah declared, `We have water of a gall to drink because we have sinned against the Lord' (Jeremiah 8:14).

"Second, bitter waters may come through other people. Joseph is an example of this type of suffering. Through no fault of his own, Joseph was sold into Egypt by his brothers, imprisoned falsely because of the accusations of Potiphar's wife, and forgotten by those he helped in prison. The actions and sins of others brought bitter waters into his life. The same may be true for you.

"But listen to his response. Joseph said:

> *Now therefore be not grieved, nor angry with yourselves, that you sold me here; for God sent me before you to preserve life...so now it was not you who sent me here, but God. (Genesis 45:5, 7)*

"We view suffering through human reasoning. By every standard of human reasoning the cross of Jesus was a waste of a great and noble life. But in the reasoning of God, it was the salvation of man.

"The same is true of Joseph. As we view him in prison, we say it is a great waste of human potential. But God was working in the midst of bitter waters. Joseph would bring life to the nation of Egypt.

"Third, bitter waters result from the circumstances of life. This is illustrated by the experiences of Naomi recorded in the book of Ruth in the Bible. Naomi experienced the death of her husband and sons.

"Until Jesus returns and the final enemy of death is conquered, death is part of life. Death entered through the original sin of man and it is a natural circumstance which we all will face, for `it is appointed unto man once to die' (Hebrews 9:27).

"When Naomi experienced these difficult circumstances of life, she said, `No longer call me Naomi (which means blessed), but call me Mara.' The name 'Mara' means 'bitter'. Naomi was experiencing bitter waters.

"Fourth, bitter waters result because of your ministry for the Lord. The New Testament speaks of suffering for His name's sake (Acts 9:16); in behalf of Christ (Philippians 1:29); for the Kingdom of God (2 Thessalonians 1:5); for the Gospel (2 Timothy 1:11-12); for well-doing (1 Peter 3:17); for righteousness sake (1 Peter 3:14); as a Christian (1 Peter 4:15-16); and according to the will of God (1 Peter 4:19). We are actually called to suffer and to respond appropriately to it (1 Peter 2:19-20). Not a message we really want to hear!

"The Apostle Paul is an example of suffering resulting from ministry. Some people view suffering as a sign of failure or lack of faith. If this is true, then the Apostle Paul had no faith and was the greatest failure in the history of the church.

"Paul said that while in Asia he was so utterly crushed that he despaired of life itself (2 Corinthians 1:8). He presents a different image than that of a cheerful evangelist who promises believers nothing but peace and prosperity.

"When Paul was first called of God to ministry he was told of great things he would suffer for the sake of the Lord (Acts 9:16). Paul's response to suffering was to endure the loss of all things to win some for Christ. He wrote to believers `to you it is given not only to believe, but to suffer for Him' (Philippians 1:29)*. Paul was not alone in suffering for ministry. The whole church suffered in New Testament times (Acts 8). Hebrews chapter 11 records the cruel persecutions which they endured.

"Many of these men and women of faith were delivered by the power of God. Prison doors opened and they walked out. They were sentenced to death in fiery furnaces, but emerged unaffected by the flames.

"But some of these believers, who are also called men and women of faith, did not receive deliverance. They were imprisoned, afflicted, tormented, and even martyred because of their testimony for the Gospel (Hebrews 11:36-40).

"We focus on living faith, but God also reveals His power in dying faith. This is a faith that stands true in the bad times, not just in good times when mighty deliverances are manifested.

"The Bible describes the attitude we should have when we suffer as a believer:

> *If anyone suffers as a Christian let him not be ashamed, but let him glorify God in this matter... Therefore let these who suffer according to the will of God commit the keeping of their souls to Him...as unto a faithful Creator.*
> *(1 Peter 4:16,19)*

"Fifth, bitter waters are a result of direct satanic activity. This is evident in the story of Job. God's testimony of Job was that he was a righteous man (Job 1-2).

"Job was a wealthy man with many blessings, but he lost it all during a lengthy spiritual battle. As he was facing bitter waters he questioned, `Why is life given to the bitter in soul?' (Job 3:20). You may have felt the same way.

"Sometimes all that a man has is in the hands of Satan. The question is then raised, will you serve God on the basis of who He is and not what you receive from Him? Will you still serve God if there are no benefits attached? Will you serve God simply because He is God?

Wrong Responses

"We have identified five ways bitter waters enter a believer's life. One of these is through your own sin. There is only one solution for bitter waters caused by sin, and that is repentance. Only when the errant Jonah repented of his disobedience were his bitter waters made sweet.

"But what about bitter waters caused through no fault of your own? What is your response to bitter waters caused by others, because of your ministry, through the natural circumstances of life, or due to direct satanic attacks? How do you respond to bitter waters for which you are not responsible, for which you can see no visible meaning and purpose? First, let us look at some wrong responses to bitter waters:

"Bitter waters tempt you to murmur and complain. When the nation of Israel faced bitter waters they murmured against Moses (Exodus 15:24). This is a common response when we face suffering. We dwell on our circumstances. We blame others and murmur and complain.

"Complaining is different from honest questioning. All murmuring is actually against God who is taking all of the circumstances of our lives, both bad and good, and using them to accomplish His purpose:

> *And we know that all things work together for good to those who love God, to those who are the called according to His purpose. For whom He foreknew, He also predestinated to be conformed to the image of His Son, that He might be the firstborn among many brethren.*
> *(Romans 8:28-29)*

"God is using every circumstance of life to conform you to His image. When you complain against any of these things, you are actually complaining against God and His work in your life.

"Bitter waters trouble and defile you. Paul warns believers to beware lest...

> *... looking carefully lest anyone fall short of the grace of God; lest any root of bitterness springing up cause trouble, and by this many become defiled. (Hebrews 12:15)*

"If you ingest bitter waters into your spirit, they will not only affect you, they will also trouble and defile those around you.

"Bitter waters prevent you from hearing from God. God sent a message of deliverance to Israel through Moses but...

> *'...they did not heed Moses because of anguish of spirit and cruel bondage' (Exodus 6:9).*

"When you are bitter in spirit, you cannot hear from God. Your bitterness drowns out the message of deliverance. The work of God's grace in your life is limited by your bitterness. If you are bitter and unforgiving towards others, then you are providing an opportunity for Satan to gain advantage in your life (2 Corinthians 2:10-11).

"Bitter waters foster a vengeful spirit. When the warriors of Israel lost a great battle, they wanted to take revenge on David. They talked of stoning him because the enemy had defeated them and taken their possessions (1 Samuel 30:6).

"Bitter waters result in depression and discouragement. Jeremiah wrote of these responses to suffering:

> *And I said, My strength and my hope have perished from the Lord; Remembering my affliction and my misery, the wormwood and the gall. My soul still remembers and sinks within me. (Lamentations 3:18-20)*

"Bitter waters poison you. Peter told Simeon he was in the gall of bitterness (Acts 8:23). *'Gall'* means poison. The Bible uses the wormwood plant as the symbol of bitterness. In the natural world, the liquor made from this plant leads to mental and physical deterioration and death. It is a natural analogy of what occurs in the spiritual world. Deuteronomy 29:18 cautions against the spiritual root that bears gall and wormwood.

"These are all wrong responses to suffering. They are the devastating results of bitter waters which are not dealt with properly."

Proper Responses

"What is the proper response to bitter waters? Let us return to the text of this message. When Israel stood at bitter waters, Moses...

> *... cried out to the Lord, and the Lord showed him a tree. When he cast it into the waters, the waters were made*

sweet. There He made a statute and an ordinance for them, and there He tested them... (Exodus 15:25)

"In Isaiah we read...

> *And there shall come forth a rod out of the stem of Jesse, and a branch shall grow out of His roots; And the Spirit of the Lord shall rest upon Him, and the spirit of wisdom and understanding, the spirit of counsel and might, the spirit of knowledge and of the fear of the Lord...and He shall not judge by the sight of His eyes, neither reprove by the hearing of His ears. (Isaiah 11:1-3)*

"When you stand on the banks of bitter waters, you must respond spiritually as Moses did in the natural world. You must cast in the Branch. You must take action to sweeten the waters.

"The Lord Jesus Christ is that spiritual Branch which must be cast into the circumstances of your life. He is represented by the tree on the bank.

"God did not lead you to bitter waters to drink of them. He allowed them for the same purpose as He did in the lives of the people of Israel. He allowed them to prove you, to see whether you would drink of the waters or sweeten them through the Branch of the Lord Jesus.

"You do not face bitter waters alone. The Bible confirms that `in all our afflictions, He was afflicted' (Isaiah 63:9). God sends no shallow sympathy card. He suffers alongside as you suffer, and there is a healing branch on the bank beside those bitter waters.

"You cannot face bitter waters on the basis of the natural sight of your eyes and the hearing of your ears. You cannot understand suffering by just what is seen in the natural world. You must face bitter waters through spiritual insight given by Him who does not 'judge after the sight of His eyes or reprove after the hearing of His ears.' Look beyond what is happening in the natural world to what is going on in the spiritual world.

"God did not cause your bitter waters, but He will redeem the negative circumstances. To redeem something means to 'buy up of each opportunity, turning it to be the best advantage'. What the world views as an ordeal, God views as an opportunity.

"He is using this opportunity to prove you, and your bitter waters will be made sweet as He takes that which the enemy intended for evil and turns it to good.

"The real test of your spiritual maturity is how you respond in the day of distress:

> *If you faint in the day of adversity, your strength is small. (Proverbs 24:10)*

"Do you consider yourself a helpless victim of fate or a man or woman of faith, whose life is controlled by God?"

Positive Purposes

"There is always divine purpose in suffering. Here are some positive spiritual results of bitter water experiences.

"At bitter waters, you your faith is tested. Everything in the spiritual world is based on faith. This is why the strength of your faith must be tested:

> *That the trial of your faith being much more precious than of gold that perishes though it be tried with fire, might be*

found unto praise and honour and glory at the appearing of Jesus Christ. (1 Peter 1:7)

"It is a trial of faith when you pray, as Jesus did, for God to let the cup of bitterness pass from you and yet you are forced to drink deeply of its bitter waters. But faith will learn that your prayers are not unanswered just because they are not answered the way you want.

"At bitter waters, you learn not to trust your own natural resources. Paul spoke of the purpose of his sufferings in Asia:

...In Asia we were pressed out of measure, above strength, insomuch that we despaired even of life; But we had the sentence of death in ourselves, that we should not trust in ourselves but in God who raises the dead.
(2 Corinthians 1:8-9)

"You may feel spiritually devastated as you face bitter waters, but...
...we have this treasure in earthen vessels, that the excellency of the power may be of God, and not of us.
(2 Corinthians 4:7)

The Apostle Paul took pleasure in infirmities because it allowed the strength of God to be manifested in his weakness (2 Corinthians 12:10).

"At bitter waters, positive spiritual qualities are developed. There are greater objectives in suffering than simply being relieved of it. The Apostle Paul said:

We glory in tribulations, knowing that tribulation produces perseverance, and perseverance character, and character hope... (Romans 5:3-5)

102

Peter declared that after you have suffered awhile, God will make you perfect, establish, strengthen, and settle you (1 Peter 5:10). These qualities conform you to the image of Jesus, which is God's plan for you (Romans 8:28-29; Hebrews 2:10,18). The Prophet Isaiah speaks of affliction as bread and water--like spiritual nourishment (Isaiah 30:20-21).

"At bitter waters, the works of God are manifested in your life. When the disciples saw a man who had been blind from birth, they asked who was responsible for his condition. Was it the sin of his parents or those committed by the man himself? Jesus answered:

> *Neither this man nor His parents sinned, but that the works of God should be revealed in Him. (John 9:3)*

There is a greater purpose than being delivered out of every difficulty you face. The greater goal is to display God's glory in the midst of your suffering and in spite of your suffering.

In the midst of intense suffering in the Garden of Gethsemane as He prepared to face the cross, Jesus cried out to His Father who had the power to allow His cup of suffering to pass. But the Father chose not to do so. It is difficult to trust the Lord when you know He has the power to change things, but chooses not to do so because He has a greater plan to manifest His works in your life.

"At bitter waters, the power of God is perfected through suffering. God told Paul...

> *"My grace is sufficient for you, for My strength is made perfect in weakness." Therefore most gladly I will rather boast in my infirmities, that the power of Christ may rest*

upon me. Therefore I take pleasure in infirmities, in reproaches, in needs, in persecutions, in distresses, for Christ's sake. For when I am weak, then I am strong. (2 Corinthians 12:9-10)

"At bitter waters, all that is unstable is removed from your life. God permits...

...the removal of those things that are being shaken, as of things that are made, that the things which cannot be shaken may remain. (Hebrews 12:27)

"Everything that can be shaken in your life through suffering is natural. That which cannot be shaken is spiritual. During the storms of life, everything that is not built upon God and His Word crumbles and collapses (Psalms 119:89 and Matthew 7:24-27).

"At bitter waters, God changes your focus from temporal to eternal. When you experience bitter waters, you often focus your attention on cause and effect. You are concerned with what caused the difficult circumstances and the terrible effect it is having in your life. God wants to change your focus from the temporal to the eternal:

For our light affliction, which is but for a moment, is working for us a far more exceeding and eternal weight of glory, while we do not look at the things which are seen, but at the things which are not seen. For the things which are seen are temporary, but the things which are not seen are eternal. (2 Corinthians 4:17-18)

God works in your affliction when you focus on eternal benefits rather than the present circumstances. Trials and problems in life are not unusual or without purpose:

Beloved, do not think it strange concerning the fiery trial which is to try you, as though some strange thing happened to you; but rejoice to the extent that you partake of Christ's sufferings, that when His glory is revealed, you may also be glad with exceeding joy.
(1 Peter 4:12-13)

If we suffer, we shall also reign with Him...
(2 Timothy 2:12)

God wants you to become a better person through your sorrows, not a bitter person. When bad things happen, don't try to blame others, bad luck, or God. If you can't fix the problem, fix your attitude towards the problem. You can change your attitude to view problems as projects; tragedies as triumphs; adversities as adventures; stumbling blocks as stepping stones; and sorrows as servants. Do not view God from the perspective of your circumstances. Look at your difficult circumstances from God's perspective.

"At bitter waters, your old self-nature is changed. God said of the nation of Moab:

Moab has been at ease from his youth;
He has settled on his dregs,
And has not been emptied from vessel to vessel,
Nor has he gone into captivity.
Therefore his taste remained in him,
And his scent has not changed. (Jeremiah 48:11)

"Because Moab had not experienced the adversity of spiritual pouring and stirring--an analogy drawn from what is necessary to develop good wine--the nation did not change. Because the people were at ease and settled in prosperity, they did not properly develop and mature spiritually. As a result, there was no positive change in their lives.

"Suffering rids you of the old self-nature. As you are stirred, troubled, and poured out, your spiritual aroma changes from carnal to spiritual.

"At bitter waters, you are chosen by God. You have asked to be used by God. You desire to be more like Jesus and have prayed to be a chosen vessel for His use. God answers your prayer through bitter waters. It is through affliction that you are chosen by God: *"...I have chosen you in the furnace of affliction" (Isaiah 48:10).* Unrefined silver cannot be used in a beautiful vessel or in jewelry (Jeremiah 6:30). Jesus said that if you are to follow Him, you must embrace the cross: *"...Don't run from suffering. Embrace it. Follow me and I'll show you how" (Luke 9:23, MSG).*

"At bitter waters, you are prepared to comfort others. The Apostle Paul wrote:

> *Blessed be the God and Father of our Lord Jesus Christ, the Father of mercies and God of all comfort, who comforts us in all our tribulation, that we may be able to comfort those who are in any trouble, with the comfort with which we ourselves are comforted by God.*
> *(2 Corinthians 1:3-4)*

"When you share God's comfort with others you...

> *...lift up the hands which hang down, and the feeble knees; And make straight paths for your feet, lest that which is lame be turned out of the way; but let it rather be healed. (Hebrews 12:12-13)*

Sometimes you may feel like you are too broken to comfort others. At those times, it might be well to remember what Jesus did the evening before His crucifixion. Despite the agony He was facing, He washed the disciples feet, served them supper, and shared words that would comfort them after His death.

"Because you have experienced suffering and you have learned to cast Jesus into your bitter waters, you can help others who face similar difficulties. You can help them get a fresh grip on life and set paths for their feet where even the spiritually lame, regardless of their circumstances, can follow. God explains precisely how to comfort others. Comfort is found in words--His Words: *'Wherefore comfort one another with these words' (1 Thessalonians 4:18).*

"At bitter waters, you will enter into a new spiritual dimension. Job was a righteous man. He did not suffer because he had sinned, as his friends claimed. They believed if Job repented, his circumstances would change. These friends tried to make a universal application based on individual experience. It would be similar to saying that because God delivered Peter from prison He will do the same for everyone. This is not true. Many have been martyred in prison despite their great faith and sinless lives.

"We must be careful when we view the suffering of others that we do not accuse them of sin, faithlessness, or unbelief. The Bible does teach that a sinful man reaps a bitter harvest because of sowing in fleshly corruption (Galatians 6:8). But sowing and reaping cannot be used to explain the suffering of the innocent. The premise is okay; the conclusion is not.

"Job did not suffer because of anything he had done. Job was a righteous man. This was God's testimony of Job, Job's testimony of himself, and his reputation before man. Yet even this righteous man entered into a new and positive spiritual dimension through suffering.

"There are four important truths revealed by Job's suffering that will enable you to experience a new spiritual dimension as a result of your own trials of faith.

"*The first is that behind every circumstance of life there is a spiritual cause.* We must view bitter waters not in terms of what we see in the natural world, but in terms of what is going on in the spiritual world. It was said of Christ that He did "...*not judge after the sight of His eyes, neither reprove after the hearing of His ears" (Isaiah 11:3).*

"In the natural world, man would say it was a terrible accident that the roof fell in and killed Job's children. They would blame the Chaldean forces for seizing his herds. They would attribute his skin infection to allergies or a virus.

"We often deny the sovereignty of God by our very words. 'Tough luck,' we say. 'How unfortunate.' 'What a tragic accident.' These terms all imply that we are victims of circumstance. But there are no accidents in the lives of believers. Our world is not out of control. Our God is the sovereign Lord over every circumstance.

"If God is truly sovereign, and the Bible confirms that He is, it means He is in control. There is no luck, no fortune, no accident. He directs your life and limits all that touches you.

"Behind the scenes in the spiritual world was the true cause of Job's bitter waters. There was a spiritual battle going on over the heart, mind, and allegiance of Job. It was also a battle between the forces of Heaven and Hell. There is warfare going on in the spiritual world over you also. That battle is manifested in the difficult circumstances you experience in the natural world.

"Remember: Behind every natural circumstance you are now facing there is a spiritual cause.

"The second truth evident in Job's suffering is that nothing can enter the life of a believer without God's knowledge. God does not cause your suffering. It is inflicted by Satan, but its limits are set by God. The parameters of Satan's attacks were set by God (Job chapters 1-2).

"The third truth evident in Job's suffering is that it is not wrong to question God. Throughout his suffering, Job questioned God as to the cause of his bitter waters. It is not wrong to question God. Jesus knew the purpose for which He had come into the world was to die for the sins of all mankind, yet in His hour of suffering He cried out, `My God, My God, why have You forsaken me?' It is what follows the questioning that is important. His next words were, `Into your hands I commit my spirit.'

"Despite his questions, Job's response was...

> *Though He slay me, yet will I trust Him...*
> *(Job 13:15)*

> *For I know that my Redeemer lives, and that He shall stand at the latter day upon the earth: And after my skin is destroyed, this I know, that in my flesh I shall see God.*
> *(Job 19:25-26)*

"After all the questioning is finished, the emphasis must change from *me* to *Thee.* You must commit your suffering, with all its unanswered questions, into the hands of God. Like Job, you must commit your bitter waters to the Lord and worship Him in the midst of your difficulties.

"We question suffering because we feel we must understand something in order to accept it. But lack of understanding does not prevent good to come from that which we do not understand. We may not understand the principles of electricity when we switch on a light, yet we benefit from it.

"When you face bitter waters, you think you have a right to know why and that you would be able to understand if only the reasons were revealed. Both are incorrect premises. Knowing does not guarantee understanding and knowledge is not synonymous with acceptance.

"If you can totally understand a thing, you have mastered it. If you could totally understand God and all He permits to occur in your life, then you would become as God. The very first temptation of man focused on this level. 'You will be as gods...You will know all things,' Satan promised.

"Our problem is that we are still on this quest for the knowledge of good and evil. We are controlled by the power of reasoning, trying to explain with natural answers that which can only be discerned spiritually.

"When you face bitter waters, do you seek the answers or Jesus, who is the Answer? The Bible says:

> *Trust in the Lord with all your heart; and lean not unto your own understanding. (Proverbs 3:5)*

> *It is the glory of God to conceal a thing...*
> *(Proverbs 25:2)*

"God may reveal some of the purposes in your suffering, but it is possible you will never fully understand your bitter waters. The things of beauty may remain hidden behind the thorns of life. The Bible says:

> *The secret things belong unto the Lord our God; but those*
> *things which are revealed belong unto us...*
> *(Deuteronomy 29:29)*

"There are some secret things that belong only to the Lord. As Job, you may never understand all the purposes of your suffering. But you do not have to desperately seek to find meaning. You do not have to justify the actions of God before the world.

"Just because you do not see meaning in the natural world does not mean there is no purpose to your suffering:

> *Since the Lord is directing our steps, why try to understand*
> *everything that happens along the way?*
> *(Proverbs 20:24, The Living Bible)*

"Life will not always make sense to you, but just because it doesn't seem to make sense does not mean that there is no meaning.

"When God finally talked with Job, He used several examples from nature which Job could not explain. God emphasized that if Job could not understand what he could see in the natural world, he certainly could not understand what he could not see in the spiritual world.

"When Job faced God, it no longer mattered that he did not get an answer to his questions about suffering. He was in the direct presence of God, and that experience left no room for anything else. He was no longer controlled and tormented by human reasoning. He replaced questions--not with answers--but with faith.

"The fourth truth emerging from Job's experiences is that through suffering, he came to know God more intimately. At the conclusion of his horrendous experience, Job declared:

> *I have heard of You by the hearing of the ear: but now my eyes see You. Wherefore I abhor myself and repent in dust and ashes. (Job 42:5-6)*

"Some of us have only a secondhand knowledge of God. When we are experiencing the blessings of life, God is often a considered a luxury instead of a necessity. But when we have a real need, God becomes a necessity.

"Job came to know God more intimately through bitter waters. Before he suffered, Job knew God through theology. Afterwards, he knew Him by experience.

"Paul expressed a similar desire when he said:

> *That I may know Him, and the power of His resurrection and the fellowship of His sufferings, being made conformable unto His death. (Philippians 3:10)*

"You can only come to know God in resurrection power through the intimate fellowship of suffering. There are lessons that only pain and suffering can teach.

My Search Of An Answer

At this point in the message, I began to share the story of Michelle and the details of her short life and sudden death.

I shared the confusing feelings, the anger, and the frustration caused by these bitter waters. I told of the day in the berry patch when God had spoken of "hidden beauty beyond the thorns" and I had misinterpreted the revelation. I had begun a pursuit of purpose and understanding to try to vindicate and validate Michelle's death.

"I felt I must justify the actions of God in permitting this tragedy," I explained. "I sought for meaning and purpose, but found no great purpose in the natural world that could justify her death.

"But I found something greater as I began to cast Jesus into the situation. I never found all of the answers that I sought, but I came to know Jesus, who is the Answer, in a more intimate way through the fellowship of His suffering. Faith became stronger than intellect and it was no longer necessary that God explain or justify her death.

"As Job, when we come to know God intimately through suffering, we see ourselves as we really are and are forced to deal with our issues. We no longer have a secondhand knowledge of God. That face-to-face encounter with God does what arguments and discussions cannot do.

"When Job stood before God, he received no new answers. He was given no new facts about his suffering, but he replaced questions with faith. It no longer mattered that he did not get an answer to his questions. It did not matter that he would not be able to grasp the answers if he had them all. Job had been in the direct presence of God, and that experience left no room for questions or doubts. Job had cast the rod of God into bitter waters."

At this point in the message, I stopped abruptly. A special anointing of the Holy Spirit was hovering over that conference room.

Something profound was happening in the spirit world...

Healing Of The Nations

The presence of God suddenly flooded that packed seminar room. All over the congregation, women were weeping. There was an electrifying sense of the presence of God. I made a simple appeal.

"I do not know what type of bitter waters you face today. You, too, may have lost a loved one. You may have been deserted by your mate or be facing divorce. You may be facing financial ruin or a doctor has told you there is no hope.

"I do not know what the first act of casting in the branch will be for you. In my case, it started with writing a letter. Your act of casting in the branch may be an apology to someone or contacting someone you have not spoken to in years. You may need to ask for forgiveness or forgive others who have hurt or abused you.

"This I do know, if you will come and cast that rod of the branch of Jesse, the Lord Jesus Christ, into those bitter waters, they will be made sweet."

Then I waited. From all over the room, women began to move forward, weeping as they came.

Rev. Juanita Smith, co-pastor of West Adams Foursquare Church in Los Angeles, came to the platform where I stood and through the gift of prophecy, the Holy Spirit finished the *"Bitter Waters"* message:

> *The Spirit of the Lord says, behold, I have been a forerunner before you and I have shown you how to deal with Bitter Waters. For I also was tempted in every point such as you, yet without sin.*

I was a man as you, even though I was God. I, too, was tempted to drink the Bitter Waters:

-When I came to My own, and My own received Me not.

-When I came to heal, and they tried to kill Me.

-When I came to give them life and they were trying to give Me death.

-When I came to reconcile man back to God and I was refused.

-When I was trying to tell them I was of God and they said I was of the Devil.

-When I came to bring them the truth, and they called Me a liar.

-When I came to bring them from the depths of Hell, and they wanted Me to experience Hell here.

-When I came to destroy the works of the Devil and the Devil tried to destroy Me.

-When I came to the end of My time and I was stretched between earth and heaven. And yet here, man comes and brings Me gall to drink But when they lifted up that gall to My mouth, I tasted it in My mouth, but I did not drink it. I refused to drink that bitter water.

And when in your circumstances the bitter waters come, you will just have a taste in your mouth. But don't drink it, don't drink it. Don't drink that bitter water. Refuse it...refuse that water.

> *-You may think you have a right to drink it, but don't drink it.*

> *-It may cause you temporary relief, but don't drink it.*

> *-It may ease your pain temporarily, but do not drink it. Refuse it.*

Maybe you have not drunk it, but you have thrown yourself in the midst of it. You are wading around in that bitter water. You thought you could sweeten the waters. You thought you could help it. You thought you could change it.

But I say unto you, stand on the banks of it, look up and look out and see Me. I am the one and I will show you what to do. It will be born of the Spirit and not the flesh.

It will not be the work of a man. It will not be the work of a woman. It will not be conceived in your own heart. But I will teach you a more excellent way because the way that seems right to man will bring you death.

Stop looking to Me and saying, `You do something.' I say unto you, even as unto My servant Moses, I am looking to you and telling you what to do. Do it with the rod of My authority.

And the Lord says, it shall not be days, it shall not be months, it shall not be years, but the instant that you fully obey Me, when that rod hits the water, a miracle shall take place.

Then Rev. Smith walked over to me, and the Lord continued to speak through her:

> *And the Lord shall use this message and it shall bring healing to the nations. It shall bring healing to the nations.*
>
> *Yes, not only the fellowship of My suffering, but the power of My resurrection shall flow through you. The spiritually dead shall arise and the bonds of the enemy shall be broken as you articulate this word.*
>
> *And it shall be a revelation that shall increase, and shall ever increase, and indeed, the shackles shall be broken and an army shall rise up because you have obeyed.*

Among those at the altar was a lovely black woman who had been abused by her father as a child. She also had a deep resentment against white people. That morning she cast in the rod, the branch of the Lord Jesus Christ, and the waters were made sweet.

There were women who held resentments against husbands who had deserted or divorced them. As they forgave, bitter waters were made sweet.

One woman admitted, "I was not only drinking bitter waters, I had cast myself into the midst of those waters. I was literally engulfed and swimming in bitter waters."

During the coming weeks, requests from all over California came in for me to share the *"Bitter Waters"* message. Each time the message was given, the same anointing of God rested upon it. Michelle's spiritual harvest was coming in!

Through the ministry of audio and video recordings, the message was reproduced and began its healing work...

...To the parents whose oldest son had shot and killed their youngest son.

...To the mother and child who were attacked and shot by a crazed truck driver.

...To the family whose two sons were arrested for murder and given life sentences.

...And to hundreds of others.

The *"Bitter Waters"* message was not conceived by studying Bible commentaries. It was not created in homiletically correct form. But then God never said it was great oratory which would bring in the harvest. He said:

> *They that sow in tears shall reap in joy. He that goeth forth and weepeth, bearing precious seed, shall doubtless come again with rejoicing, bringing his sheaves with him. (Psalms 126:5-6)*

The passage says *"He that goeth forth weeping,"* not "he that goes forth preaching great sermons." You can learn in the crucible of suffering what you will never learn in the pages of a textbook, a commentary, or by years of seminary. When you are weeping is the time to sow.

Just one month after God spoke the promise that it would bring healing to the nations, the *"Bitter Waters"* message was on its way to South Africa. There, this message which had been born in the spirit of a white woman, ministered to a black man whose only son had been shot and killed by white men.

On the verge of suicide, this man played the Bitter Waters sermon tape over and over again. Then he laid aside the sleeping pills he had planned to take. Instead of death, he experienced new life through Jesus Christ. Today, he serves as a minister of the Gospel.

The healing of the nations had begun.

A Message From Michelle

I was pushing the shopping cart down the aisle of the store, when I spotted a trinket on the sales counter.

"How cute," I thought. "I'll get it and save it for Michelle when she comes in the spring."

Then the horrible realization swept over me. Michelle would not be coming in the spring.

I pushed my cart on down the aisle. As I turned the corner into the next aisle, I saw her. Could it be?

Yes, it was Michelle! She was dressed in a beautiful dress of pure white, her face wreathed in smiles, and she was walking towards me.

I ran to her and hugged her. "Oh Michelle, I am so glad to know you are all right! Now that I have you, I do not want to ever let you go again."

"But Aunt Patti," she said. "You don't understand how beautiful it is here. You don't realize what it is like."

"Are you happy?"

"Oh, yes, Aunt Patti."

"Michelle, do you know really how much I love you?"

"Yes...I love you too...I'll see you in the spring."

As suddenly as she had appeared, Michelle was gone. Then I heard a voice say, *"She came willingly."*

Abruptly, I awoke. It had been a dream. Through it, God had permitted Michelle to come to me with a final message.

I remembered the words spoken by Rev. Roppe at Michelle's memorial service:

> *Michelle knew what it was to present her body to Christ a living sacrifice. She gave it willingly. God receives Michelle's sacrifice.*

So it was true. She had gone willingly. Had God shown her in those final moments of life the great impact her story would have on the nations of the world?

I believe so, and she chose to go willingly in order to bring in a harvest through her death that would have been greater than that in her lifetime.

Someday I will round the aisle of this mortal life, leaving all the earthly trinkets behind, and I will see Michelle in the spring of eternal life.

I have a final message from Michelle to you who stand at bitter waters. The Sunday prior to her death, Michelle attended church as was her custom. The sermon topic was "Life" and the text was from Philippians chapter 4.

After her death, we found the notes Michelle made during that service:

Life
May 18, 1986

The gift of life is to see another day. We need to be thankful for life. God gives us peace and understanding in the face of violence like killing and terrorism.

But do not think on these things. Think on things that are true, lovely, and praiseworthy. God gives us strength. He supplies all our needs. Learn to handle everything, no matter what.

...I have learned in any and all circumstances, the secret of facing every situation. I have strength for all things in Christ Who empowers me. I am ready for anything through the strength of the one who lives within me.

When Michelle made these notes, she did not know that before the week was up she would face death. She did not realize that there would be those left behind who would struggle with understanding the violent incident which took her life.

But she encouraged us to learn to handle everything, no matter what, and to accept the gift of life in each new day. We must achieve peace and understanding in the face of that which is unacceptable, replacing unanswered questions with confidence in a sovereign God. And this can only be done through the strength of the Lord Jesus Christ.

God wants you to learn to handle everything, to face every bitter circumstance of life and, through casting in the rod of the Lord Jesus Christ, see your bitter waters changed to living waters.

You cannot face death until you first learn to handle the circumstances of life. Michelle's last words to hospital attendants were, "Tell the police it was an accident."

She did not ask how badly she was hurt. She did not blame Seth for his carelessness in handling his weapon. In her final moments, she cast the rod of love and forgiveness into bitter waters..."Tell the police it was an accident."

Michelle learned to handle life through the strength of Christ who lived in her. Because of this, she was ready and able to face death.

You may have been drinking bitter waters for years. The roar of these waters in your anguished soul may have drowned out the voice of God. You may have murmured and complained, questioned and doubted. You may be totally consumed by bitterness.

During your life you will face bitter waters repeatedly in different circumstances, but remember: God has not led you to bitter waters to drink of them. The Bible says, *"Let bitterness cease."* Each time you face bitter waters, you must cast in the branch, the Lord Jesus Christ.

Numbers 5 records an interesting Old Testament practice used when a woman had been accused of adultery. She was given bitter water to drink. If she was guilty, the water would enter her system and kill her. If she was innocent, the bitter water would not affect her. Only through the righteousness of the Lord Jesus Christ can you face bitter waters. Without Jesus, you will ingest bitter waters spiritually and die.

When Jesus ate the Passover meal with His disciples, Judas left after tasting the bitter herbs. He never experienced the bread and wine shared by the Lord Jesus Christ and his life ended in tragedy.

You, too, have tasted the "bitter herbs" of life, but you must not stop there. Go on to partake of the body and blood of the Lord Jesus Christ. If you do not know Jesus Christ as your personal Savior, God's call to you today is...

> *Ho, Everyone who thirsts, come to the waters, and you who have no money, come... (Isaiah 55:1)*

Jesus declares:

> *...Whoever drinks of this water will thirst again, but whoever drinks of the water that I shall give him will never thirst. But the water that I shall give him will become in him a fountain of water springing up into everlasting life. (John 4:14)*

Do you have unanswered questions? Are you hurt and brokenhearted? Have you been rejected by friends and family? Have you drunk deeply of life's bitter waters? God wants to substitute living water for bitter water: "*He who believes in me, as the Scripture has said, out of his heart will flow rivers of LIVING WATER*" *(John 7:38)*. God will bring you through those bitter waters:

> *When you pass THROUGH THE WATERS, I will be with you; and through the rivers, they shall not overflow you... (Isaiah 43:2)*

> *He sent from above, He took me, He drew me out of MANY WATERS. (Psalms 18:16)*

> *...We went through fire and THROUGH WATER, but You brought us out. (Psalms 66:12)*

A Message From Michelle

"If my lifeblood must be poured out for a sacrifice to God to nurture your faith, I rejoice for myself and rejoice with you all...
Likewise you also should be glad and rejoice with me,
And congratulate me on my share in it."
(Philippians 2:17-18)

JESUS, HE IS THE ONE
By Michelle

The flowers in the meadows, The gardens, the fields,
Are full of sparkling colors, Their fragrance so real.
But I know of one Flower, Who surpasses all these ones,
Whose beauty is beyond description, He is the perfect one.

He is the Rose of Sharon, He is the Christ of God,
It is Jesus our Savior, His beauty is so pure.
There are the stars of Heaven, They twinkle, Oh, so bright,
Their lofty place in the heavens, Lifts our eyes on high.

There is a Star who shines,
Much brighter than the heavenly host.
His brightness far surpasses
What human eyes have known.

It's Jesus, our Savior, He is the bright and morning Star,
Who fills us with His glory, And shines in our hearts.
The sun rises up to heaven after a cold and frosty night,
And sends her rays of comfort to warm us with delight.
But there is a Son of righteousness, with healing in His wings,
Who gives more light than the sun on earth-
It's Jesus Christ, our King.

He is the Son of righteousness, He is the King of heaven,
He gives us light, He gives us love,
He fills us with peace and joy from above.
He is the beautiful one, He is the perfect one.
He loves you and through His love we are united as one.
If you are looking for love and light,
For beauty and fulfillment, Then look no farther,
Oh wandering one--Come home to Jesus,
He is the perfect one!

EPILOGUE

As this third edition of "Bitter Waters" goes to press, many years have passed since Michelle's "graduation" day. Through the continued distribution of the "Bitter Waters" message, Michelle's story has greatly impacted the nations of the world exactly as prophesied.

I have personally witnessed her spiritual harvests throughout the United States, Africa, Asia, and from the steaming jungles of Trinidad to the frozen Arctic region of northern Russia. Her story has been told repeatedly behind prison bars and it has penetrated death rows. The "Bitter Waters" message has been translated into several languages, distributed through audio and video, and aired nationally on radio and television.

Over the years we have received numerous letters from people whose lives were greatly impacted by Michelle's story, confirming that through her sacrifice "she, being dead, still speaks" (Hebrews 11:4).

In 1995, Michelle was reunited with her mother--my sister Cathy-- who slipped suddenly from among us to join her in Heaven.

If you are like me, you will not face bitter waters only once in a lifetime. Over the years since the writing of this book, I have lost my mother and father and faced the diagnoses of dementia in the lives of several precious friends and family members. I have lost great spiritual mentors in my life--some through death, others through moral failures. I was part of a great church where a crazed shooter entered the building one Sunday morning and killed two young ladies and wounded three others. Repeated waves of Bitter Waters.

In every situation I have faced and am facing, I have found that this message of "Bitter Waters" has brought emotional strength and spiritual healing. The message continues to bear fruit that remains in my life and--through Michelle's story--in the lives of countless others.

When my time on this earth is concluded, I will join Michelle in a place where only sweet waters are permitted to flow--for in Heaven, there shall be no more Bitter Waters.

I will see Michelle in the spring again, just as she promised.

-The Author

THE BITTER WATERS MESSAGE...
FRUIT THAT REMAINS

*Thou hast taught me, O Lord, that our work need not end
when our days here come to a close;
its impact can outlive the hands that perform it.*

*In fact, much of the world's work is done by those who have
already departed, for we live by the afterglow of the fruitful
days they spent here.*

*When I see lives interrupted, I am tempted to say,
"For what purpose is this waste?"*

*Help me then to remember that afterglow.
Let me recall that among the forces of earth none is more
potent than that produced by those who we call "dead."*

-George Mathewson

Royalties from this book are being donated to:
Harvestime International Network
For the healing of the nations-For fruit that remains.
http://www.harvestime.org